Dating While Feminist

Essays on Sex, Dating, and Feminism

Victoria Young

A HEART ON PAPER PRESS ORIGINAL,
DECEMBER 2023

Copyright © 2023 by Victoria Young

All rights reserved. No part of this book may be used or reproduced in any manner whatsoever without written permission except in the case of brief quotations embodied in critical articles and reviews.

Published in Canada by Hearts on Paper Press LLC, Vancouver

Paperback ISBN: 979-8-398-14386-7

WRITER. DATER. MASTURBATOR.

DATING WHILE FEMINIST

This book is dedicated to vibrators.

DATING WHILE FEMINIST

Victoria Young is a writer whose
work you can find in bookstores and on the internet

www.victorianachos.substack.com
www.instagram.com/victorianachos

DATING WHILE FEMINIST

OTHER BOOKS AVAILABLE BY VICTORIA YOUNG

Love Poems For Butchers

DATING WHILE FEMINIST

DATING WHILE FEMINIST

DATING WHILE FEMINIST
ESSAYS ON SEX, DATING, AND FEMINISM

Victoria Young

DATING WHILE FEMINIST

CONTENTS

A Man Wants to Fuck you
1

On Fatness
3

Homecoming
7

Young Men Without Substance
15

This is All My Fault
20

Frogs in Training
27

Angry Men Are Exhausting
42

An Olympic Minute
49

A Tale of Three Andys
55

On Romance
86

First Date Magic
91

Closure for Dummies
103

Stuffed Chicken and Tossed Salad
111

Poker Face
118

Good Vibrations
131

The Chosen One
138

Knowing About Fat Girls
147

Girls Just Wanna Have Dessert
157

Beauty Fades but Red Flags Are Forever
166

The Perfect "No"
173

A Tad Abrupt
177

Election Night 2016
187

A Nashville Twin
192

Misgivings in Memphis
198

Louisville Slugger
213

The Loophole
221

DATING WHILE FEMINIST

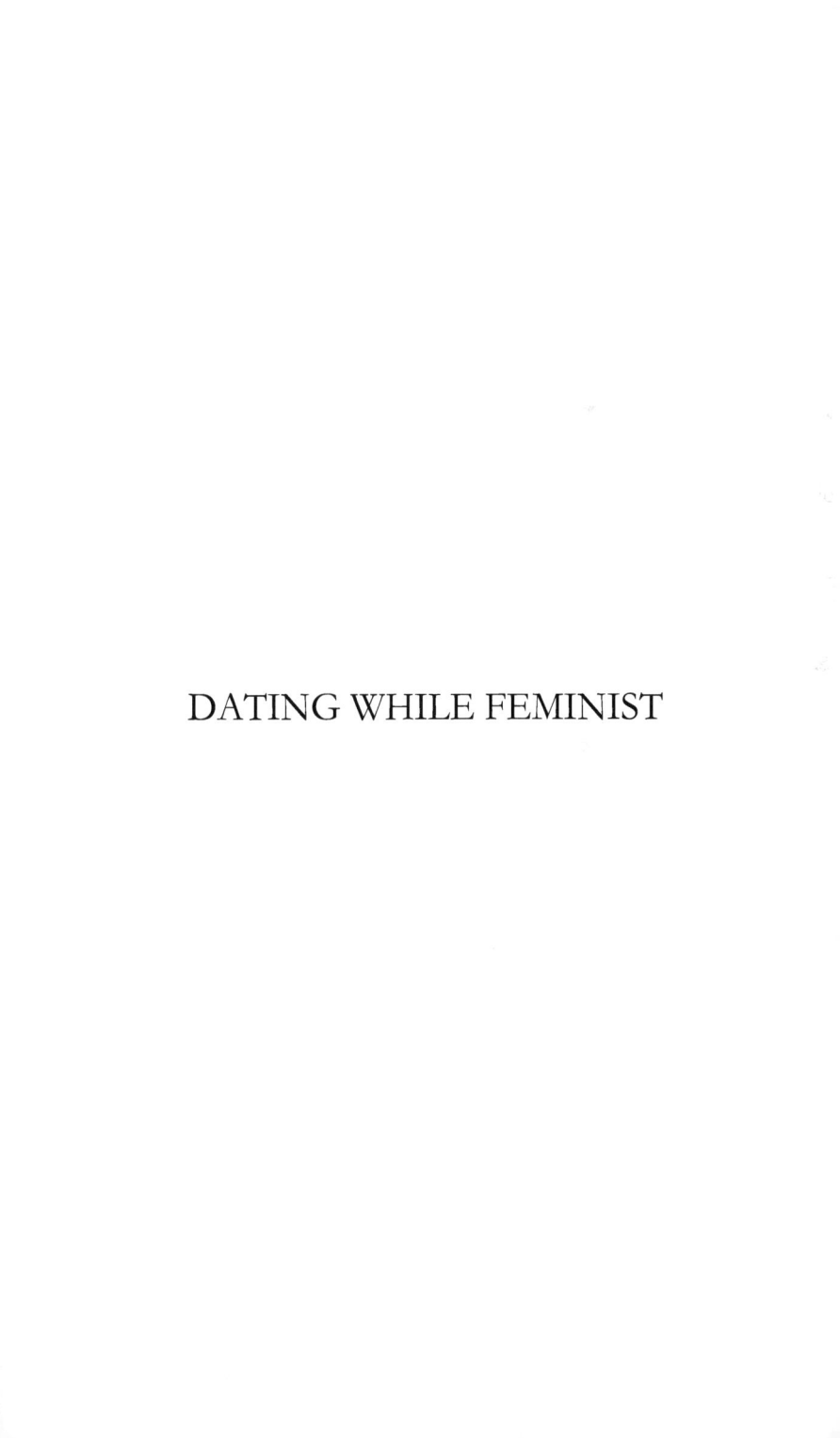

A MAN WANTS TO FUCK YOU

I can't believe I used to think online shaming was wrong. Now I think anything short of tattooing men with the things they've said to me is injustice.

      A man on a dating app messages: "Now you have some gorgeous DSLs," and I think they should write DSL over his lips. Make him answer the question a thousand times, "What are DSLs?" Make sure his mamma asks him. Make him say the words: Dick Sucking Lips.

      A man messages: "That cleavage shot…amazing." Stamp it across his forehead. Make sure his family asks over the holidays just exactly why he felt his voice was worth sharing, why he reduced an entire photo to the crack in my chest. Leave him forever marked by the way he views women.

      A man messages: "I wanna fck u," and leaves out all the wrong things. Tattoo that on his face. Tell the world this stranger wanted to fck me. Make it so every employer will ask, "How much tho? How badly?" Make sure it follows him forever. Men love an easy escape, a lack of evidence, a violence that draws no blood. He should spend his life hemmed in by the very idea that he thought a stranger wanted to hear what he wanted to do to her—unprovoked, unasked for.

A man on a dating app will tell you, too soon, whether or not he wants to fuck you because he thinks you want to know. Before ever asking you much of anything, a man will tell you he wants to fuck you, it having never occurred to him that you have value outside your pussy. Men will fuck a couch, a hole in a wall, a woman he loathes and still be under the impression that his sexual interest is interesting. He never connects the dots. Men live for sharing their opinions, but a man's attraction is not a compliment. A man wanting to fuck me is not a compliment. I am far greater than his boner will ever know. *His* desire, *his* attraction—they're about him not me. The focus is always just a little off. Do not listen to men who speak so freely about your body. Let their desire fall at your feet, worth less than the dirt on your boots.

ON FATNESS

I need to find a way to tell you that I'm fat. In this story that is about me, but also about you because none of us are truly that unique, I need to find a way to tell you that my lower belly bounces and hangs against my thighs. Uncaged by a bra, my breasts sway when I walk; my flesh is more than the average; my sweat pools in beautiful creases.

    This story is not about my fatness but when you live as a fat woman, everything is about your fatness. You either fit in with society or you don't and when you're fat, nothing fits. You never fit anywhere, that's kind of the point. In fatness, you are excluded. But you're never just one thing. I am fat, and I am also a woman, and when you're a woman, everything is about your fuckability. The world will tell you your only value exists between your legs and in the circumference of your waist. But the world is stupid. Outside in the world, Fatness will be at the intersection of your suffering, but inside your home, inside your heart where the spaces become safe and fat liberation spreads through your veins, your fatness will be nothing. But you cannot stay inside forever, and so we have to talk about your fatness, my fatness. As a fat woman, the world will tell you that you're both unfuckable (because you're fat) and also only worthy of being fucked (because you're fat). None of this is new information if you're fat like I'm fat. You've spent your whole life being fetishized by men for your width and breadth. The majority have no idea the depth you possess.

In these stories about sex and dating, I have to find a way to tell that you that I am dating while fat, I am dating while female, I am dating while feminist. In this story that is not about my fatness, I need to find a way to tell you that sometimes men treat me terribly because I'm fat and sometimes they treat me terribly because I am a woman. But those are all excuses for them. We can give their hatred a path, a box to be categorized into, a place to feel the specific hurt, but there's a bigger truth to it all.

When men treat me terribly—when men treat *you* terribly—the blame belongs at their feet not ours. Men who enact harm on others do so out of weakness, an inability to process the expectations of the outside world alongside their desires. Not all men, of course (God, I hate the impulse to have to say this).

Sometimes, men treat me terribly because I'm fat. They treat another one of us terribly because she's Black. Another still is treated terribly because she's disabled or queer or trans or ugly or because they met her on her most vulnerable day and spot an opening that can be taken advantage of. They treat us terribly because society told them it was okay to do so, and we endure it because society told us we were weaker or strong in the wrong way or a fetish or a thing not a human, divisible into all our parts or whatever specific slight you carry in your heart that is but the tiniest part of you.

And so, my fatness both matters to the story and doesn't matter at all. I am fat. I am a woman. I am straight in a way that makes suffering at the hands of men a near-certainty. I need to tell you that I'm fat, so it takes the sting out of it for you, so that you can focus. So that you know that there's no power in the word and there's no power in their hatred. I need you to know that their opinions about us our worthless. Truly, undeniably, and without justification, absolutely worthless. The only opinion that matters is your own. I want you to know I'm fat because I'm not ashamed of it (even if you or they think I should be).

I want you to know that I'm fat. I *need* you to know I'm fat, but not in the way that you know it. I'm not fat and sad or fat and angry or fat and worthless. I'm just fat. Everything else stands on its own. If I'm being honest, my body is absolutely the least interesting thing about me, but that doesn't mean I don't love it.

I love my body because it's a body and its mine and my love of it needs no justification. And when I write a story about the sex I had or the way I see the world, I need you know I'm fat because that matters for context but then I need you to immediately forget it because we have much more important things to talk about—like the way men treat women. Because even though I think men will hurt us all in our own specific ways, I think their mistreatment of us is because we're women. Their weapon of choice is simply the easiest one to grab that day. It's why a man can be chatting you up one minute and hating you the next.

Upon getting a rejection from me on a dating app, a man does an about-face to spit, "fuck you fat bitch," in my general direction. He says fat because he thinks it'll hurt the most (and for some women it will) but I know his hatred lies most heavily in the *bitch*. He hates me because I'm fat and I've rejected him, but his sense of entitlement is in the fact that I'm a woman and the rage that follows because I have dared to not want him. He doesn't see me as a human being because I am a woman, hasn't learned that I am a thing of value, that I am a beating heart inside tender flesh. I need you to know I'm fat because the world will never let me forget it, and so neither should you. But it's not the whole story—It's not even the best part.

HOMECOMING

"What should we tell them you're doing?" my mother asks over the phone.

It is the summer of 2014 and my last month in Montreal—the first time—the time I'm there for grad school. I am thirty-two years old and moving back to my childhood home (the place I have spent all my in-between years, all the figuring-it-out spots in my resume and my life). My mother expects me to have a real game plan. Expects might be too strong of a word—hopes. Together, my parents hope.

I have a master's degree now and a plane ticket home, and I think I have a plan, but I do not really have a plan. I have optimism and arrogance which can serve you well or ruin your life—it's luck of the draw. I have this dream that I'll write a book, and someone will want to publish it. I don't dare think about whether or not anyone will buy it. I have a thousand things to say, some of which I'm certain are worthy saying. I have the naïve belief that this is what I was meant to do. I have the desperate need to make a difference in the lives of others. Maybe I have nothing at all. It's too hard to say in this heat. Salty confidence drips down my back.

"Tell them I'm sweating," I joke. When you're fat, everything is always damp and just a little bit funny. Tell them that it's hot here, what with the humidity and the dating eighteen-year-olds, and the terrible fear of never amounting to anything. The pressure to know my next step is barometric, oppressive, suffocating. Make a joke on my behalf. Tell them that you were kidding about their ages. Say, "She was just making a joke." Say it laughing, "Never younger than twenty-one, that's gross."

Dad chimes in on the phone (you must have it on speaker) and asks if age is searchable, asks if there is a box to check on the apps so I can stop collecting youth. He says it as a joke, and I tell you both that it's not me. I say, "I haven't searched for shit." I look at my face in the mirror to see what young men must see: a leg up, a time capsule, discount Valentine's Day chocolate. I say nothing.

Mom says, "I've been telling them that you're writing and handing out resumes."

"Good," I say, "That's the truth." I reassure my mother that they can be proud of me now, their daughter with three degrees and no job lined up. How many degrees do you have to earn not to feel like a loser? She reassures me that they've always been proud. I know it to be true even if I'm not sure I can be so proud of myself. Earning a master's degree (in the arts, no less) at thirty-two doesn't feel as bona fide as it should. I know people my age who own homes.

Tell them that if a writer dies in the forest everyone hears it, but if I die in an apartment building it's just called a sublet. Tell them that that you're joking. Tell them that the famine is over. Tell them not to worry anymore. Stand in a coffee shop, on a golf course, at the Greek restaurant I bussed tables at when I was sixteen. Tell them that I'm sweating. Say "It's the best summer ever." Say it loud and use your hands "BEST! SUMMER! EVER!" Say it again, no need to worry anymore (hand them my resume).

Tell them that I'm Hemmingway until I remind you how much I write about handjobs. Tell them that I'm Dostoyevsky's right hand, jacking off Kerouac. Say, "You're going to change the world," and mean it. Say it again. Use the Meisner technique. Say it until I believe you. When I'm hanging up the phone, whisper it again. Hope for osmosis. Hope for happiness. Hope for someone, maybe, just a little bit older.

Before I hang up, Dad sneaks in, "Don't forget to at least look for jobs in Vancouver." I must've scared him a bit with all my talk of moving to Romania or up north. I probably wasn't serious, but you never know with me. One day I'm filled with fear and the next day the adventure starts. Brave and anxious in equal measure.

Tell them that I'm sweating. Tell them not to worry. Hand them my resume.

The summer after earning my master's degree was light as lint. I breathed with ease; I was optimistic and certain. The future seemed so effortless and guaranteed. I would be somebody now. I had done a thing of worth. But that's not how life or worth works. Someone has to see value in you for you to have worth (your value is constant and of your own making but your worth—that's something the market decides). The market for moderately educated fat women is not nearly as thriving as you'd think. It doesn't matter if you're talking about my career or my dating prospects—the results were the same, no one was buying.

July came and I left. I packed what I could fit into two suitcases (and two boxes to ship) and sold everything else on craigslist (at rapidly declining prices directly linked to my terrible fear that I wouldn't be able to get rid of it all before I left). By the final week I was basically giving it away for free (insert metaphor for my sex life). Nobody told me that I could just leave whatever I hadn't sold in my apartment. Nobody told me that because you didn't pay a deposit you could just up and leave, no fucks given. Instead, I let a string of strangers into my apartment for five bucks here (a lamp) and ten bucks there (my printer). I gave all the fucks I had stressing myself out so completely that I developed shingles two weeks before heading home. It was an absolute nightmare which, honestly, seemed a fitting way to leave Montreal. When I landed in Vancouver, my dad picked me up at the airport. Driving back to my parents' house, in the town I had grown up in, I swore I wouldn't stay long.

"A few weeks, maybe a few months," I said, "Just until I figure things out."

Swiping right on Tinder, in my childhood bedroom, I felt like a real hero, a champion of the no-shame brigade, a real fucking patriot. I mean, do you understand the level of courage it takes to be a full-grown adult, swiping right on Tinder while back in your childhood bedroom on people you went to high school with (or theoretically worse the younger siblings of people you went to high school with)? Do you understand the level of confidence and lack of self-doubt that takes? Was

I strong of character or a beacon of chaos, honestly it was a bit hard to tell at the time but what was the worst that could happen?

Three days later my dad had a heart attack.

Sitting in the front seat of the car that day, and every one that followed, it seemed much harder than it should be to breathe. "Stress," is what my mother said. "Completely understandable."

"Is it though?"

I wasn't sure what I deserved to feel. After all, my heart wasn't the one under attack. My Dad has and will always be one of the great lights of my life and while I've always known that the death of my parents would happen one day, his abrupt heart attack really put it all at the forefront of my mind. I just had to keep reminding myself that he was okay. The Doctor put in a stent, gave him some meds, and that was it—we all just carried on. Because he was okay. The next question was whether or not I would be?

Every new match on Tinder seemed to ask the same questions.

How was your weekend? Any big plans? Get up to anything fun this weekend? and I didn't know how to say, *my dad had a heart attack, and I am now completely untethered* but like, without being a bummer, so I just unmatched them. One after another, I matched and then unmatched. Until there was enough distance. Until the question had a better answer. Until I could breathe in the front seat of the car.

He showed up wearing white nurses' sneakers, which wouldn't have been so bad except that it was the first disappointment of many—strike one. I couldn't help but wonder if some of the disappointment was my fault—If I hadn't maybe gone into our first date high off of my experiences in Montreal. Come to think of it, maybe my experiences in Montreal weren't even that great, but that in the rosy glow of hindsight I had made them all feel impressive than they were.

    We met for coffee, and he showed up looking like someone had let all the air out of all his pictures. This was my first date back in Vancouver and it was an absolute garbage fire (minor hyperbole). If it sounds like I'm being too harsh (I am), I want you to consider a few things about first dates. I want you think about how much things like effort and risk are gendered. When a woman goes on a first date, she's risking her safety (and her sanity) and the effort it took to make herself presentable (by the standards of our modern patriarchy). I want you to think about the expectations placed on a woman showing up to a first date, and whether or not a man has similar expectations live up to. A man will show up to a date wearing cargo shorts. A woman could never.

    I once wrote an article about how the reason I think (nay, demand) men should pay on the first date (and if they know what's good for them, several more) is because of the financial investment women are forced to make in our appearances. The cost of makeup, pink tax on razors and shaving cream, the disgusting price of bras (especially if you got big knockers and especially ESPECIALLY if you're also plus-size), to name a few. Then there's the waxing appointments and the hair styling that for some reason always costs us more, not to mention the gender pay gap. This is all to say that even showing up to a date puts women financially and emotionally in debt, so if a man is not paying on the first date he can absolutely get fucked (but not by me).

He had originally suggested we meet at a Tim Horton's and I'm Canadian but I'm not *that Canadian,* so we met at Starbucks. When he showed up wearing space boots and cargo shorts, I couldn't help but think about how much I had prepared for this date: strapping myself into an uncomfortable bra, putting on a full face of makeup, styling my hair (using the eight or so products it takes to tame my curls not to mention at least a half hour of flipping and defusing and scrunching and whatever the fuck magic it takes to appear decent looking). I had done all that *and* driven the half hour it took to meet in his area. So, when you hear me describe his appearance with sharp judgement and no time for bullshit, I beg of you to have a little empathy for what I'd already been through up to this point.

A first date is supposed to be your best foot forward and here was this young dude showing up with his chicken legs in shorts and goddamn pillows on his feet while I looked adorable and perfectly put together (obviously I'm biased but whatever you're on my side so just believe me). First dates are for appearing impressive and fuckable—and let me tell you, no one has ever gotten wet for clown shoes and cargo shorts.

We stood at the counter ordering our drinks, and he ordered hot chocolate, which is a stupid thing to be bothered by, but it served to remind me that I was now on a date with a child who had tried to convince me he was a man and it had me thinking I was about to be his mentor rather than have good time. Strike two.

We sat at a booth in the back (because I was already dying of embarrassment and wondering how long exactly, I had to stay before I could end the date).

I was sipping my coffee thinking of how to salvage this date when I noticed his fingers, which were all sporting big hunks of gold.

He noticed my glance and offered, "They're hockey championship rings."

I leaned in, finally something intriguing to get us back on track. "You play hockey?" I asked enthusiastically.

"No."

I stifled an awkward laugh of dismay. "Then why do you have the rings?"

"I had them made," he said like that wasn't totally bonkers.

"You just…had them made…for yourself?"

He nodded without even the tiniest hint of embarrassment or awareness. I drank my coffee so fast it burned my throat. Strike three—this date was over.

Space boots texted later to see if I wanted to hang out again. Of course, I didn't, which I thought would've been clear by how short our date was, but I shouldn't have been surprised by his lack of awareness, after all this was a man making awards for accomplishments that weren't his.

I often wonder how men end up this way—is it just simply because they're male and straight and the world is mostly handed to them on a platter, so they never learn about social interactions and how little they have to offer? It made me think that perhaps he'd been on hundreds of other dates where things had gone smoothly so that now in this aberration it didn't even occur to him that he'd have to be intelligent and charming and fun. It never even occurred to him that he'd have to read some body language and signs. All my signs were stop.

DATING WHILE FEMINIST

YOUNG
MEN
WITHOUT
SUBSTANCE

I find it bizarre the way anyone could think I seek out younger men. Younger men have almost nothing to offer. A fact that has never stopped even one from messaging me.

You into younger guys? They ask sheepishly (at least that's how I read it). I can't stand a tepid man. The joke is that they're often barely younger than me—a man of thirty-one once messaged to ask if I was interested in a *young stud*. Insert vomiting noises. It was truly bonkers behavior given that I was only two years old than him.

Some of the men who message me are genuinely younger—usually in their early twenties—which at least gives credence to the question though still makes it idiotic to ask. I wonder if they think me too stupid to have seen their age in their bio. Sometimes I wonder if it's all in an attempt to be fetishized, but women don't care about that shit. We care if you're hot. We care if you have energy. No woman has ever told her friends how great it feels dating a young guy simply because he's young. We're not men, and you can't force someone into fetishizing you (though I'm sure they'd try if they could).

The truth is most often they're asking because they want to highlight the age difference, they want it made clear that they are young and thus not looking for a relationship (which makes even less sense once you've talked to some forty-year-olds on the apps because let me tell you sister, they probably don't want a relationship either). I'm not bothered by their lack of interest in a relationship, though I'm never not baffled by the audacity it must take to feel the need to say it right up front, as if they genuinely thought I was dying to fall in love with them.

You into younger guys? They all ask, never once expecting anything but an enthusiastic yes to their question.

Not especially I answer back because I can't bring myself to get it up enough to lie to them.

Barely, is what I'm thinking.

Only on a good day, I want to write.

Probably not is closest to the truth.

Depends on if they're awesome or not, is what I usually say.

I feel like I'm screaming into the void. Young men haven't a clue and honestly that's kind of embarrassing for me because I guess it's my job to carry us both on this adventure but I'm tired and mostly bored by them. The only thing young men have to offer is enthusiasm. And there's a fine line between enthusiasm and obnoxious and let me tell you most young men don't know where that line is. Everything else with them is a burden.

The mythos of the young man and the MILF has been designed by and for the male gaze—movies produced by men, tv shows written by men, men greenlighting book deals. Our entire society believes in the mythos of the cougar and then young stud (but only for sex, of course). Now, don't get me wrong, has there been an occasional *young stud* (I'm using their corny language here) who has graced my bed and truly proven himself to be worthy? Yes. But those men, the kind of young men hot enough to warrant the time it takes to train them, those men with the genuine willingness and self-awareness to know their place and what they have to offer, those young men are few and far between. So, when I say I don't really like younger men, I'm not lying. Even though I keep going out with them. They are not who I would design if I had the chance. It's more coincidence than purpose, I assure you.

And yet, how do I keep ending up with so many young men in my inbox? *Society*, I mumble under my breath. The truth is, at the age of thirty-three, there just aren't as many single men as you'd expect there to be. Plus, of those single men, they must be attracted to fat women in general and me specifically, and they have to be interesting to me or exceptionally hot (note: they're rarely either), and then it's preferable that they're not looking for a relationship but also that they respect and value women beyond their bodies (which is beyond-fucking-impossible-to-find). The truth is there aren't that many options for a single, fat, thirty-plus-year-old, educated, intelligent, and feminist cishet woman who wants to actually date men not just have unsatisfying sex with them for validation.

A man online says, "All due respect but those boobs," then a hearts-for-eyes-smiley-face, and then two hands clapping. He says, "Older women help me fulfill my total potential." He thinks this is charming. When I am offended, he says, "Well, it's just the facts, you are older." I read it with intonation. I read it like it's new information.

You ARE older.
YOU are older.
You are OLDER.

He waits for a response. He doesn't know that I'm already bored with this. He doesn't understand that I am horrified by his lack of awareness. He has never even considered what it is that he has to offer. Spoiler alert: It's nothing! He offers me nothing. He is without an offering.

Why am I always expected to provide, to be something, to give of my body and my mind. Smile for them. Make them laugh. Show them your body. Not too much too quick though. Give them everything they want. Be kind. Be pleasant. Be a thing worthy of their idiotic conversation, their tedious ill-thought-out plan. Have they ever considered that they might be unloveable, unlikeable even? What it must be like to be a man! A medium ugly man with enough audacity to topple a skyscraper wants to use me to fulfil his total potential. Why does no one ever think about my potential?

THIS
IS
ALL
MY
FAULT

After space boots (whose real name I can't remember), I go out with Cody who tells me he's twenty-five but turns out to very much not be twenty-five. Everything about Cody is wrong for me. He's soft and sweet and not very smart. He sends me pictures of him working out at the gym, flexing in the bathroom, smiling into the camera. He's buff with a baby face, and because he went to the trouble of finding me on Twitter instead of waiting and hoping for a match on Tinder, I agree to one date.

    I arrive to our first date early, sit in my car, check my lipgloss and swipe on tinder. I'm only a few swipes in when Cody's picture pops up. His age reads twenty-one. I'm seething because I did my hair and I drove all this way and I hate liars. I turn to my right to see Cody excitedly waving at me through the passenger side window. *Too late now, bitch.*

Cody is the one who pursues me. Cody is the one who lies about his age. Cody is the one at fault for all of this, but somehow, I'm still the one to blame because I'm thirty-three and you'd expect someone my age to know better. But that's the thing—because I absolutely *did* know better. I just also had the audacity to think that I could orchestrate a few fun weeks out of this.

So far, my dating experience consisted mostly of first and second dates (plus two boyfriends—one short and one lengthy relationship but those both feel separate to all this, somehow). I so badly wanted to have a more fun than that. I didn't want a relationship and I wasn't interested in commitment. I just wanted to go on some dates that led to at least a few more dates before we both realized we weren't meant for each other.

Cody made me think that was possible, or more accurately, Cody's enthusiasm for me made me think that was possible. At least I think it was his enthusiasm that got me. It also could've been the fact that I was turning thirty-three in a few weeks, and nothing reminds you of your youth quite like dating one. Or perhaps it was just because I, like Cody, was an absolute idiot. I guess we'll never know.

The night of our first date, I wanted to put on a lemon-meringue pie's worth of concealer. How much makeup do you need to mask a twelve-year age difference? I had gone out with younger men before, when I had been younger still, and it hadn't seemed like such a big deal then. Now though, *now* I was over thirty.

Now everything seemed to have a spotlight on it. Now, I was a cougar. It's so embarrassing the way we fetishize age differences.

The first date turned out to be like most. We ate food, we laughed and had a good time (because I always make them laugh and we almost always have a good time). He paid (because he'd *fucking better*), and then he asked if I wanted to take a walk somewhere. I agreed before realizing that we'd be carpooling since he'd taken the bus to our date. Ooph.

The date had actually been pretty fun so far, lying and age-issues aside. His enthusiasm for me had a real alluring quality to it. So, I agreed, and we drove to the Quay to go for a walk. While trying to pay for parking, the machine didn't seem to be working. Before I could offer a better solution (any solution would be better than what he did), Cody was shaking and banging the machine like a wild animal, or a twenty-one-year-old, I guess. I yelled at him to stop it and a loud siren emanated from the machine. Mortified, I quickly wrote a note about the broken machine and left it inside my car like an adult (even though I now very much felt like a teenager).

We walked along the quay and my blood pressure lowered. Cody was just so sweet—like a golden retriever—and because neither of us lived alone (which seemed normal for someone his age and abnormal for someone mine)—we made out in public. He kept stepping on my white maxi dress and, I kept wishing we were somewhere else, somewhere inside, and private. But his lips were nice, and it was fun and *christ* he just seemed so eager.

The date unraveled the way all fairy tales unravel—like a math problem. I offered to drive him home (and that's my bad), and he accepted, which meant

I had to drive another twenty minutes in the opposite direction of where I lived (which was 30 minutes away to begin with). Ten minutes from his house he asked if we could hit the drive-thru at McDonald's, which had to have a been joke but wasn't. He was dead serious. Something about it being his "cheat day" and not having eaten enough at the restaurant earlier. Not one to expose my binge habits to others, I ordered nothing and just listened as this dude rambled off enough for three people and then looked at me all sheepishly with puppy-dog eyes and shrugging shoulders like, "I just like to eat." Outside his house, but still in my car, we made out again, this time surrounded by the sweet aroma of fresh fries. With Cody's tongue in my mouth, I was already emailing my brilliant marketing campaign to McDonald's in my head.

Driving the fifty minutes home, I found myself thinking maybe it hadn't gone so bad, after all maybe this is what dating a twenty-one-year-old looked like—heavy on both the babysitting and seduction.

The next day Cody texted repeatedly. He wanted to know how I was doing and how my workout went and what was I up to. He wanted to talk, even though we didn't really have that much to talk about.

I had a really great time, he messaged.

So did I, I texted back.

The following day was the same and the same the day after that—a lot of interest and nothing of substance. I wouldn't say that he was losing his appeal, but my enthusiasm was cooling the more aware I was that neither of us lived alone (and weren't likely to be changing that scenario anytime soon).

Cody starts sending me pics every day. At first, he's just shirtless and showing off his muscles from the gym, which admittedly are still covered in a layer of cuddles, and I can't help but wish that every thirteen-year-old girl had the blind body-loving confidence of men. He doesn't have a model body. He doesn't even think about not loving it. He sends pictures of it regularly and without request.

I find the messages kind of intrusive until it occurs to me to make a request. First, I tell him that I won't be sending any of me. I want his expectations tempered. I need to make sure he understands that there will be no equal exchange. Because I am a writer. Because I want to be famous. Because I simply don't want to. Because I can't risk it. Because I don't trust him. Because the year was 2014 and times were different. There are a million reasons.

I understand he types.

He sends me a dick pic. I hate dick pics. I've never seen the impersonal, unexperienced, theoretical image of a stranger's dick and thought anything other than what is this fucking idiot doing sending this garbage to me. To me, a dick is an extension of a man I like, not a reason I like a man. A dick is nothing on its own. A dick is no island.

Instead of shutting him down though, I start making requests—*send one of you smiling,* I say and then add, *send me a video.* The video is exactly what you'd expect, it's all dick and stroking and nothing else and though I recognize his dick and body from the earlier pictures, it could really be anyone in that I feel no connection towards it, so I up the ante. *Send me one where I can see your face.*

A video arrives of him touching himself while he thinks about me. He's looking into the camera (at me) knowing that I'll be looking back at him. I feel powerful for having asked for it, and for having the appeal to command such a request. Once again, my interest is piqued. Now I want a second date. Now I care that this thing doesn't end right away.

He seems more invested as well. *What else do you want?* he asks, and I tell him. I want a video of him talking to me while he jerks off. I want to be a part of the film, even in absentia. I want his desire for me memorialized. I want to keep it forever. When we're over, I want to have a piece of him, a piece of his desire for me, locked away. Just because. For my ego, or my memory, or because it helps with closure, or just as a reminder. I want to keep a piece of all of them. This will be his piece. He sends the video. The next time he asks me out, I say yes.

I say yes to the world's worst second date idea. I am ashamed even typing it out here—but I have to because it's the truth and that's what we're doing here. But know that it takes me hours to do it, it takes hours (months, years even) to admit that on one particular weekend when my parents would be out of town, I invited him over to their house, to my childhood bedroom, where I was currently living as a thirty-three-year-old degenerate. In my defense (I'm an idiot), everything seemed to be going great. He kept saying how much he wanted to spend time with me.

The night of our date, I drove to pick him up at the Skytrain station and brought him back to my place. We ate pizza and watched the Hobbit and had entirely mediocre sex, and then he spent the night which I hadn't really thought through and was definitely a huge mistake. In the morning, before I had to drive him back to the Skytrain station, he told me that he didn't think we should see each other anymore. He said he didn't really think we had anything in common. I couldn't believe he was telling me this in person instead of via text after dropping him off at the Skytrain. His crime was not the rejection (I was hardly bothered by that, after all he was absolutely right in that we had literally nothing in common). Forcing me to spend the next forty-five minutes with him *after* being rejected by someone I was barely into was a crime that deserved death. I'm already swiping on Tinder before the weekend is over.

After it's over with Cody, I spend a lot of time thinking about the sting, the rub, the hurt. I'm acutely aware how little the feeling has to do with Cody himself. The feeling is because I am the one to blame. He shouldn't have gotten sex as a reward while being so undeserving. I couldn't seem to wrap my head around it. I knew that there had to have been a moment, or moments, where I could've been smarter, done it better, made it happen. But I was not smarter and so this is my fault. I worry that I'm starting to sound like psychopath. I'm not sad because he left. There is no sadness in his rejection.

He said, "I have a stronger connection with someone else," and of course he did, I mean OF COURSE HE DID. He thought I wanted something big with him but truthfully, I just wanted laughter and kissing and fun (which, in hindsight he wasn't even providing). Nonetheless this is now and that was then, and back then (and still a bit now) I struggled with the idea of how quickly men figured out they weren't interested in continuing to see me. Was I just a nightmare of a person or was it the men I was dating? I spent a lot of time think it might actually be both.

FROGS IN TRAINING

"What kinds of qualities do you look for in a woman?" I ask. I am running through the last of the typical getting-to-know-someone questions. This falls somewhere after, "Whereabouts do you live?" and before, "What are you looking for on here?" though honestly, they're all pretty interchangeable.

He says, "Confidence," and I hate him almost immediately on principal. The attraction to confidence is reasonable enough but if you were to ask most men why so many women lack confidence, they rarely have even the smallest understanding of their own role. And yes, I know, not all men but enough men, surely too many men. I can't help but hate these men—the men who talk about how much they love a girl who eats freely and openly in front of them, a girl who doesn't have issues with food, a girl who isn't a real fucking drag. Those men hate my fat body. It's always the same men who say that a woman shouldn't wear so much makeup, or doesn't need to wear it at all, as if they should be anything other than silent about the ways in which women try to protect ourselves from the brutality of this world. Those men, so many fucking unaware men, who complain about the phenomenon of "duck lips", as if they weren't the reason that women get lip injections and make that stupid face, pouting our lips like ducks desperate for approval, desperate to be sexually attractive. As if the typo wouldn't be a more accurate description: dick lips.

"I like a girl with confidence," he says, and then later when rejected, "Whatever you fat bitch, I wouldn't have fucked you anyway, I just heard fat chicks suck good dick." I can practically hear him singing "Fatty fatty boom-boom latty," which is a real shame because I love a good rhyme. I can hear him from a mile away. His words are so loud I can hear them from the future. "I like a girl with confidence," he says without even a hint of awareness.

This is what dating is like when you're fat. This is what dating is like when you have even a lick of sense. After you learn about men, dating them becomes so terribly embarrassing. This is why I need you to know what it's like on the apps so that you have empathy for all the dumb decisions I make. You'll think it's desperation or a devaluing of myself but that's not true—it's that there just aren't that many good options if you're a cishet woman and you want more in your life than friends, family, and your favorite tv shows. You'll ask yourself why I keep kissing frogs but that's because you don't know that there are easily forty more layers of filth and amphibians beneath frogs that I'm staying away from. You'll ask why I ever settle at all, why I even entertain the possibility of dating someone in their early twenties. My only answer is to gesture at the layers of disappointing men on the apps. Avoiding them is an impossibility and just when things seem at their worst, you will always manage to discover some further layer beneath that you'd never considered. Frogs are just princes in training. You have no idea what other nightmares lay beneath the moss and sludge on dating apps.

I was once in a writing workshop where two different narrators were being discussed: one, a male serial killer, and one, a single woman. Everyone agreed that the female narrator needed to be more likeable in order to get the reader on her side, and I hadn't even written her as fat yet.

"How can I be expected to write a likeable narrator when I can't even get a man to take me on a second date?"

Everyone laughs but the joke is quickly ruined because they too-easily believe my self-deprecation. It's a play on words not my heart.

Johnny broke my heart almost right from the beginning. This is hyperbole, of course. I wish Johnny could've broken my heart. Like Cody before him, Johnny was too sweet for me, by which I mean he was too young and naïve which comes off as sweet and gentle but is really just someone figuring out their life without considering your feelings. If we're being honest that's what all young people are doing (which is exactly what makes them so terrible to date). And if you're thinking, well, you're the one who's older so you should've known better—you'll get no argument here. I absolutely should've known better, which is starting to feel like a real pattern with me.

My only defense is that I've come to learn it is not age but experience that is the real teacher in life—at thirty-three, I still hadn't dated enough to know any fucking better (at least not for sure, not better enough to stop making the same mistakes over and over again).

I know better *now* but that's because I've dated all the men. Okay, so obviously not all the men but I've dated enough men that I think it's probably safe to extrapolate the data. I've seen it all. I've done it all. *I've even let a few of them do me.* I know a million more things now than I did back then, but it's worth noting that I've also dated age-appropriate men with the similar results of frustration and lack of sexual satisfaction, so if you ask me whether I want to be sexually and emotionally disappointed by someone in their twenties or someone in their forties—I'd say why not both!? Why are you trying to limit my misery! Let me be free!

The first time I meet Johnny is in the parking lot of a mall. He wants to drive on our date, but I don't want to give him my home address, so we meet at the mall like teenagers (which he not so long ago was). He drives a vintage car—Hemingway blue. I'm kidding, there's no such thing as Hemingway blue. I made that up to sound literary, to give this story credence—the mention of an old white man validates anything.

I find it hard to describe men in my writing, or more specifically the men I've met in real life, men who could potentially come across a story about them. I adamantly believe that they don't need to be protected—we, as a society, already protect the egos of men the way we should be protecting the hearts of little girls (and full-grown women), but there's something about describing someone's physicality that always feel like an insult. He was short, he was thin, he was beautiful. His body had tattoos and a youthful softness to it. I couldn't tell you what color his eyes were if you paid me a million dollars. He must've had a face, that I know for sure.

I used to try and write fiction, but the men never came out right. My thesis advisor would say, "You have to give more jokes to the men." She'd say, "They all sound so flat."

I'm tired of telling people that it's the truth. That they are, in fact, flat. I'm tired of telling people that the world of men isn't so full of brilliance. It hurts when I can convince them of the truth so quickly.

"People are the worst," they say repeating my words back to me, but being right is no conciliation prize. Men don't deserve the jokes I have written. They don't deserve the immortality of humor. They haven't earned being anything more than exactly who they are. They do not tell jokes, so I keep all the jokes for myself. They are mostly silent because they were mostly silent.

My thesis advisor used to ask for better dialogue, wanted to know what he said, wanted to hear it like she was there. But I was there, and they never say much of anything. I don't know how to tell her that it was mostly awful, that the things he said were horrible or silent. It's harder to find way to write out the silence. I don't know how to say he was boring without being boring. I don't know how to tell her that the truth refuses to be bent. I tell her that tomorrow I will try again. She asks if I mean dating or writing, and I no longer know the difference.

The last advice my thesis advisor gave me was, "You have to learn to trust your reader." But, in grad school my readers included men, the kind of men who you would've thought were feminist because they were in grad school in liberal arts, but you'd be wrong. In one workshop, a male colleague gave my submission to his wife to read and critique because it "wasn't his thing." My advisor said I had to learn to trust my reader, but the average reader is more empathetic towards serial killers than single women. Another colleague wrote in the margins, "I want to know more about the male characters, make them more well-rounded and funny." But I'm writing nonfiction and they don't deserve the credit of my jokes. He said, "I want to know their motivations." As if I could know the mind of a rapist. As if his story deserves more page space than mine. As if a woman doesn't deserve to be the protagonist of even her own life.

"I read your website," he says, and I have no idea what that means. Has he read one blog post? Has he read the entire thing? Which entries has he read? What did he know? MY GOD WHAT DID HE KNOW?!? This revelation of his was terrifying, but it was also wonderful because he must like me enough to be interested in knowing everything about me. This is the kind of naïve stupidity I used to have around men. My therapist would say that I'm closing myself off by thinking that, but that's because she's not fat, and she hasn't dated men like I've dated men. She doesn't share the lived experience of having a thousand (or maybe like thirty) men give absolute signs of interest only to immediately be proven wrong. The way I used to give credit for the most basic effort and interest from a man shocks me now. At the time, it felt like Johnny was genuinely, truly, unbelievably fucking curious about getting to know me. I was acting like he had signed up for a college course on my life instead of just doing a quick google search or two (to his benefit no less).

He'd already told me, before meeting, that he'd been able to find my Instagram and Twitter (and my website), but it was shocking how that still seemed like too much effort for most men. Cody had said that he didn't google me because he wanted everything to be fresh, to get to know me from me (as if my writing was by authored by a ghost instead of my own brain). Cody said that he wanted things to happen organically (after hunting me down on Twitter).

There was a time I might've believed that logic. Now though, it just seemed like someone who didn't have enough curiosity nor effort to get to know me. Then again, why was it so important to me that they did or that they went through the effort to find my online footprint? It's not like I had a fetish for internet sleuths. Maybe the ugly truth was that I wanted new readers rather new lovers. Either way, I wanted a man to care about what I had to say, even if what I had to say was imbedded in blog posts about sex and dating. I was never really writing about sex and dating anyway. Not really.

"Oh god," I said dramatically trying to remember everything I'd ever said about every man I'd ever dated. "I hope it wasn't too bad."

"You're really funny."

"Thanks." I breathed a sigh of relief, paused and then asked, "What made you read it?"

"I wanted to have as much information as possible," he said. "You're pretty intimidating."

"I am?" Didn't he know he was the intimidating one in this scenario. He was busy stressing about impressing me at the exact same time I was busy stressing about being a disappointment to him.

"I'm so nervous!" I was practically shouting. I was trying to make us both feel better, but I'm not sure it even moved the needle. I've always felt that there's something about verbalizing an anxiety that makes it disappear. Like, if I'm terribly nervous for a date, and I just say it to the person so that they know and I know they know, suddenly everything is a little less nerve-wracking. So, I blurted out that I was nervous and waited to feel better.

"Why are you nervous?" he asked. I was immediately nervous again.

"Because you're so young." I blurted awkwardly wishing I could melt into seat. I shouldn't have said it, but it was the truth. He was cool as shit and not a pretentious dick about it. He had tattoos he loved but could admit that some he regretted. He asked questions with genuine curiosity, and he seemed to think I was pretty adorable. When we bantered back and forth, I felt like I was funnier than usual. Maybe he could be my muse. Maybe he could my lover. Maybe we could be buddies. I didn't have a limit set on my heart. I tried not to think about our ages, but I couldn't help it. They were everything and nothing. After all, it's not exactly like I was living the life of a thirty-three-year-old. I was temporarily squatting in the home of my parents to save money while trying to live that artist dream (read: sleeping in my childhood bedroom being supported entirely by my parents while trying not to crumble under the pressure of a hundred-thousand-dollar student loan and the privilege to even think an artist-dream-life was possible). I wasn't exactly a trophy-cougar. I was a poorly aging twenty-five-year-old, which if you think about it really isn't that much older than a twenty-one-year-old. Right? *Right?!*

The truth about age is that it all starts to seem relative after a while. If you message with enough age-appropriate men, you'll find out that there's really only two kinds—those who talk about your body in invasive and gross-way-too-early ways and those who are at their core too boring for words. With those limited options, somehow an eloquent and polite twenty-one-year-old starts to seem reasonable. All of a sudden, you've got a not-corny, not-sleazy, articulate, funny, interesting guy on your hands, and who am I to be turning down such an opportunity? Doesn't everyone keep telling me to be more open and to give these guys a chance (and then later chastising me for being a terrible judge of character)? It's almost like you can't win.

In the car we laughed about our mutual nervousness, and I tried to let him convince me that I was brilliant. When he had to parallel park the car on a hill, I prayed for it to be easy. Can you imagine having to parallel park, on a steep hill, in a vintage car you've only just started driving, on a first date, with someone a decade older? I'm stressed and embarrassed just writing about it. I'd rather have a catheter inserted.

Inside the pool hall we shoot eight ball and drink sodas (because we're both sober).

"How long were you together?" I ask when the conversation turns to dating, turns to his ex, turns to this thing he has to get over.

"Three years," he says, and I do the math even though it seems unnecessary. It doesn't matter how old that made him when they met. He's twenty-one now and three years in a relationship is his entire life. It is first love and first everything. I can already see it on his face. He is broken now. Fixable, sure, but right now, one hundred percent, he is broken from this.

"When did you break up?"

"Wednesday," he says, as if I had meant the day of the week rather than the distance of time from then until now. As if we weren't on a first date only a few days after the (painful) dissolution of the most important romantic relationship of his life. I kick myself for not asking before agreeing to this date. He says it like it's no big deal. I try not to choke on my soda and look around for the cameras as I'm clearly being pranked.

"Ooph," is all I can manage to say. I want to leave immediately. I want to cry about what a waste of time this has been. But I'm an optimist, or a rescue dog, I'm not quite sure which metaphor fits best. What I do know is that in this moment, even though we're taking on water, I must not let the boat sink. Don't let this disappoint drown us, I think. Maybe I'll be his lifejacket (I mean Jesus, can you imagine the arrogance?!). But it is what I think in that moment, in the awkwardness and stupidity of it all. It is what I say to myself, leaning across the pool table, trying to take a shot, while this twenty-one-year-old tells me that he's been wrecked by a storm and I'm all: *yeah yeah, cool cool cool,* I'm sure we can find some spare driftwood around here to patch you back up good as new. I practically say the words good as new. I am an idiot in a typhoon. I still think this can work. I still think I can make this work.

We play a few games of pool, most of which I win. I can't tell if he's impressed or intimidated or neutral or upset. He seems to be having a good time but never touches me. I make movements towards him and wait. I go in three-quarters. I go in so he can come the rest of the way. He smiles and never moves an inch. We flirt or we are just two people of the opposite sex being friendly—I can no longer tell (can I ever tell? Something to think about for later).

Maybe I'm not even flirting so much as just trying to have a good time. Together we drink our sober sodas, and the bond of sobriety feels like trauma bonding over a murder. This is the first time being sober on a first date hasn't given me a twinge of guilt and shame for being the wet rag.

"No, no, you go ahead, I don't mind at all," I say as they order something alcoholic, and I mostly mean it. If they have less than three, if they don't get weird, if it makes them more fun, it's fine. But with Johnny I don't have to worry. We drink sodas and tell jokes and there's no guilt and there's no shame and we ask each other about meetings (he goes, I don't), and coping (it's a process), and then it's nothing. It's a thing that makes it so there isn't a thing between us. And it's yet one more thing that makes him seem older than he is (I'm starting to see how this could all be my fault, the blinders I'm wearing, the miscalculation of it all).

He pays for the sodas, and I let him because they're cheap and because he offers and because it seems like the right thing to do. When the games are over, he walks up to me sheepishly and confesses that they only take cash, and he doesn't have enough cash. He has some cash but not enough cash, and they don't have an ATM in the pool hall, and if I have some cash he can run to an ATM after, "or I could run there now," he offers.

I say, "No, of course not," and pay whatever he can't. It's like ten bucks and not a big deal at all and mostly I'd do anything right now to end the embarrassment he clearly feels at not having enough cash. I imagine his wallet must have Velcro on it. We pay and it's fine though the age difference seems so intense in this moment that it's a buzzing neon sign flashing between us. It's entirely illogical, but I feel like a mom who just came in and paid the bill for her son.

Things go from awkward to ridiculous on the drive home. Cruising down Oak St. towards the bridge, a truck pulls up on the passenger side and three men inside try to talk to us.

"How did you get such a hot babe to ride with you?" one of the men in the pickup truck yells, and I feel like I've just stepped onto the set of *Dazed and Confused*. Another leans over from the passenger to shout, "You should get out of that junker and ride with us!" They yell a few more derogatory things about his car and complimentary (if not objectifying) things about me, and Johnny handles his own in a manner fitting an actual grown-up (far better than I would've handled said behavior, which is mostly just to look shocked and sink back into the seat), but the awkwardness is palpable. It's like having a bunch of dudes whip out their dicks, insult each other's, and then look to you like, "Who's the real man pick me pick me?" and you're just like, uh what the fuck bros this is so gross. Except that I can't hold it against Johnny because he didn't ask to be a part of this. And then the light turned green, and they were gone, and he brought me back to the mall where my car was waiting.

It took an hour for the message to come via text, but I knew what it would say the moment we had hugged goodbye in the mall parking lot. I could feel it in his shoulders.

I'm not ready to date again. I'm sorry.

I tell him it's fine. I tell him I understand. I try not to let the disappointment, which is to be expected, plunge me into a depressive episode. I say, *keep in touch* and he says he will, and we actually do.

A few months or so later, we meet for a coffee which I think is a date but turns out is definitely not a date. We have a nice chat, we drink our coffees, we promise to keep in touch.

A few more months after that he messages me on facebook. He says something flirty that makes me think maybe he's finally ready for something to happen with us. We make plans to watch a movie at his apartment. He orders sushi, which I happily eat without worrying about judgement because I've been on two dates with Johnny and I'm not about to miss a meal for a third date that could be absolutely literally nothing. I've felt his bait and switch before. I'm not missing a meal for a man who doesn't know what he wants, that's for damn sure.

For two hours, we sit side by side not really touching, definitely not cuddling and I wait for Johnny, who had invited me over, who had expressed interest, to make a move. No move ever came. After a while I got bored, and I got tired, and I stood up to leave.

I must've taken a wrong turn. Somewhere in between leaving his place and arriving home, it all quickly turns to shit. If you meet a man at the top of a hill, things can only go down from there. Johnny and I started on Everest. The idea that there is enough joy in dating to make it worth it, that the weeks of fun will be worth the rejection that comes later was a fucking delusion. I can't help kicking myself when I'm down.

It hurts because I never seem to get the weeks. At best, I'm getting in only a few dates (and kind of shitty dates at that). This time there wasn't even a kiss. He stood in the doorframe of his basement suite, on our third date spread out over a year, and said that I shouldn't feel bad about how I look (as if his rejection of me had that kind of power) because he found me really attractive, but that he just wasn't "feeling it." I wanted to set his air quotes on fire. That said, there is a kind of painful relief in someone finally admitting that they weren't into me because of my shitty personality rather than my fat little body.

    And of course, I'm joking.

    I'm joking, of course.

    He hopes we're going to stay friends (as if). He likes my "comedy" he says. "Keep that coming," he says. And I can't really remember why I thought we should stay friends, when we never were friends to begin with. I don't know why I think we should try to be friends. I can't wrap my head around his both being attracted to me and liking me as a person but not "feeling it." I no longer understand what "it" is. Though I'm starting to wonder if "it" is definitely all my fault.

    It's almost as if dating twenty-one-year-olds isn't a good idea.

    After the rejections from Cody and Johnny, things start to get a bit darker. It's not them personally, nor is it the rejections, it's just this feeling of missing out on a future I had thought would absolutely be available to me (and it's my depression—let's not downplay that). It had never really occurred to me that it would be so hard to find a man to get to four dates with. I wasn't looking for a future, but they always seemed so scared of having one. I just wanted to have a couple fun nights, to have some tension and excitement, to have some new experiences and yet it seemed like I couldn't get past a second date or even find that many men I wanted to go on a first date with. I was thirty-three now and though I had earned all these degrees, without a steady career or a successful book, I couldn't stop feeling like I'd never accomplished anything.

ANGRY MEN ARE EXHAUSTING

After Cody and Johnny, I go on a lot of first dates that never turn into second dates. I go out with a guy named Trevor who shows up wearing jeans, a fresh white tee, and an undeniable rage seething just *barely* below the surface. He's fresh out of the military and never makes eye contact. We sit far apart on an outdoor sectional at what used to be my favorite Starbucks but is now the Starbucks where I met Trevor. We never discuss his rage *per se* but the whole date is tainted by a feeling of aggression and dissatisfaction. *His ex-girlfriend was crazy* (sir, be serious, you're talking about her to me on a first date, *she* is not the crazy one). *The military is a scam* (and I mean, hard agree, but also way too intense for a first date, not to mention he never once asked what I did for work). *People here suck* (alright sir, maybe tone it down a little or add some specifics because I am, in fact, a person who is here right now).

At one point, because I'm a fat woman who lives in a world that hates fat women, I wonder if he's disappointed and angry because I'm fat. I wonder if before the date he had romanticized me in his mind as someone smaller, more fragile. But as I stand up after this horrible date where he asks me no questions and offers me no interest, I choose to believe the better alternative. Trevor would've shown up this angry to a date with any woman.

I tell him it's getting late, which it most certainly is not. I think we hug goodbye—probably the first kind touch he's had in a while. Trevor is not my burden to carry nor my blame to absorb. Angry men are not angry because of me. It is not my job to save them. It is not my job to tolerate them. Sitting in my car, with the air conditioning cranked, I keep the windows closed. I have this sneaking feeling that Trevor is going to knock on my window and ask for a second date. Even though the date was stressful and uncomfortable for me, I fear Trevor wouldn't view it the same way. While his animosity for life was jarring to me, I can't help but assume it's his natural state. I peel out of the parking lot quickly and breathe a sigh of relief. It's such a shame, I think, aside from the anger and total lack of personality and social skills, he was a real hottie. But that's the problem (or the blessing?) with dating in your thirties or any age at which you've done enough dating and fucking that a man being hot no longer cancels out anything. Trevor texted later that night to ask me out again.

I don't think we're a good match, I wrote.

He responded with some saving-face-type-nonsense about how he completely agreed. It was bullshit but that was fine with me. I could let an angry man save face.

After Trevor, I go out with Brandon whose name I've made up because "angry coffee from Kamloops" is a mouthful and he just seemed like a Brandon (sorry Brandons). The night of our date, after I'd spent two hours doing my hair and makeup, Brandon messages to ask if I'll pick him up on the way to our date.

I cancel immediately.

Why? He texts.

Because I don't want to date a man who asks for a ride on the first date. Because I don't want to pick him up. Because I don't want a stranger in my car.

He pleads. He begs. He gaslights.

I really want to meet you, I promise you won't regret it, please it's not a big deal.

I cannot tell you how many bad decisions I've made in my life because I didn't want to waste my hair and makeup. The moment I see Brandon, I know I've made a terrible mistake.

Men should read books about women. Men should read books about fat women. And, of course, men should read this book. But if nothing else, men should read this next paragraph and really absorb what I'm saying.

It is a huge generalization to say that men lie about their height, but as any woman on a dating app can tell you, a huge number of men do, in fact, lie about their height. The same men who do this, when called out for lying, will usually begin a diatribe about how women don't like short men or how women show up fatter than their pictures showed or whatever missing-the-point-misogyny is fresh on their mind at the moment but here's the truth—women hate liars. It's bonkers to lie about your height (or misrepresent yourself in any way—don't think I'm here to defend anyone who posts inaccurate pictures on a dating profile). When you meet the other person, they're going to notice. When you said you were 5'10 and you show up eye to eye with me, I'm going to fucking notice. Furthermore, doing this immediately tells the other person that you're insecure about [insert whatever thing you hid in your photos].

The irony is that I will absolutely date a short guy. I will fuck a short guy. He still has to be awesome and everything, but height has never actually stopped me from dating anyone. Insecurities so severe they lead to misogynistic rage though?

[insert barf sounds]

Is there anything less attractive? I am not your therapist and I'm not your friend. I'm a first date and just like the anger of men, I am unwilling to carry the burden of their insecurities, now and forever. Fix your shit before the meet up time babe. Or at least understand that it's the deception and the insecurity and the lack of self-acceptance that women are really taking issue with when you show up four inches shorter than you claimed to be on our first date. Or, as in the case of Brandon, the sparsest combover I've ever seen after only posting pictures of you in hats.

Ironically, Brandon had not lied about his height. When he climbed into the front seat of my car, all 6'7" of him barely fit, as evidenced by his knees crunched up against the dashboard. Pissed about having to pick him up for our first date, and pissed about his deceptive pictures, I did what any reasonable person would do and drove us to the coffee shop for our date. Brandon, of course, doubled down on being bonkers and refused to order a drink (while letting me pay for my own). We sat in the coffeeshop as I sipped my coffee and he sipped on every last inch of tolerance I had. Brandon was as angry and aggressive as Trevor, unknowingly imitating him by talking only about himself the entire time.

I counted down the seconds till it felt reasonable to end the date. Brandon told a vacation story about swimming with sharks and every anecdote was about how important money and material things were to him. He was a salesman at heart (my least favorite profession) with the exception being that he seemed to have no ability to read his audience. It was like being on a date with Al Pacino's character in Devil's Advocate and I just kept waiting for his greasy combover to melt down his face to reveal the fiery figure underneath. No respite ever came and after about an hour I suggested we leave.

Any decent person would say goodbye at the coffeeshop and walk to the bus stop or call himself a taxi, instead Brandon followed me to my car suggesting we go back to his place to watch a movie.

"Oh, sorry I can't," I said lying through gritted teeth. I think I even faked a yawn and stretch, "I'm really tired."

"Didn't you just have coffee?"

Well, he had me there.

I didn't really care if he could see straight through my rouse though, there was no-fucking-way I was going home with this animal (minor exaggeration)—I'd rather swim with sharks.

"Yeah, I don't know why I'm so tired," I said (it was probably your terrible company and fucked up values), "just a long day, I guess."

He asked again when we arrived at my car and instead of saying goodbye, he got in. He asked again when I pulled up to his place.

"You're not that tired," he whined.

"I am," I said, further judging him for trying to convince me to do something I obviously didn't want to do. I'd spent so much of my life being pressured by men to take things further and though I'm sure I hadn't perfected the art of saying no just yet, I was getting significantly better. I wasn't about to cave for this dipshit.

Brandon remained sitting in my car staring at me so intensely I could hear it when he blinked.

"Okay, well, I have to go now so," and I gestured at the door. He finally got the picture and opened the door. I'm not even sure he'd closed it behind him before I was speeding away. At a stoplight, I rubbed at his knee imprints in my glovebox.

I would've thought that was the last time I ever heard from Brandon but shortly after arriving home he began frantically texting. He wanted to know what had gone wrong or what I didn't like about him. I lied and said it was nothing particular, just that we weren't a good match. I didn't know how to say any of the real reasons with kindness (mostly because by this point, I felt no kindness in my heart for him). If he'd asked me months down the road, I probably could've found a way to deliver the bomb softly but having only just escaped it all, I was hardly in a place to be delicate. He pushed and pushed and pushed until I finally thought *fuck it, I'm going to tell this guy the truth about himself,* and I fucking did. I told Brandon every misstep he'd made (asking for a ride, making me drink coffee alone, talking only about himself, having terrible values, being unable to read the room, requiring a ride home, harassing me until I gave him a critique), I pointed out every deception he'd offered (mainly the baldness and only having posted photos of himself in hats), and just overall let him have it. As you would expect, he acted like a grownup, took the criticism, and thanked me for taking the time to give him feedback. Just kidding, he called me a stuck-up bitch and some other nasty stuff I couldn't care less about, and I stopped responding till he disappeared.

Men stay menning, amirite.

AN OLYMPIC MINUTE

When I was back in Montreal, just after grad school, I went on a date with an Olympic sprinter. We had a great time, made out overlooking the city, made out in his car, and when he dropped me back off at my apartment, I didn't invite him up (because that was when I still thought it important not to fuck on the first date—which I guess I still do but for different reasons than I did back then). On our date, I ordered mozzarella sticks and nachos which felt revolutionary given that he was solid muscle and could run a hundred meters in... just kidding I have no idea how fast he runs. I googled to make sure he'd actually been in the Olympics (he had) and that was the extent of my interest. We texted a few times after that, but nothing ever came of it and then that was it, I had moved back to Vancouver.

So, when Murphy, my latest tinder match, told me he was on the Jamaican bobsled team, I almost laughed (how many Olympians can one girl date?). I quickly found out that he was only in town for the night, having just arrived from Whistler (where the team was training).

Tomorrow he would start his drive toward Salt Lake City (where the team was based during the season). I wasn't going to fuck him (was I?) but what harm would a quick drink do?

Normally, I wouldn't bother meeting someone who's only in town for one night (because normally they're not hot enough or famous enough or have a funny enough life story to make it exciting for me). But when you're a girl who grew up watching Cool Runnings and you get asked out for a drink by a man who is literally living the story in that movie, how could you possibly say no? You can't say no. After all, you haven't lived until you slid, amirite. And if you're thinking—is this bitch really going to tell us another story about fucking a super-hot dude? Obviously.

We met up at a pub in Richmond across from the hotel he was staying at. It was a Ramada which is a brand I always seem to confuse for Radisson which is far more upscale and bougie. Needless to say, I've never stayed in a Ramada and not been disappointed that it wasn't a Radisson (which feels like an apt metaphor for dating). The amount of mid to low-level hotels that I've fucked in throughout my life is truly staggering. There has to be someplace I can redeem my frequent fucker miles.

In his wonderfully heavy Jamaican accent, which (like an idiot) I was surprised by, he told me that the team had been training all week up at Whistler. Upon arriving at Vancouver airport, the day of their departure, they discovered some issues with the paperwork making it so the sleds couldn't be shipped home. Instead, someone would have to stay behind and drive a van with the sleds inside back to the training center in Utah. Murphy volunteered. If it wasn't so sad, the similarities between this real-life situation and the plot of the 1993 movie Cool

Runnings would be comical. But as it was, the team being so down on their luck (and low on resources) that they had to rend their sleds from another team just to practice was kind of devastating (or a triumphant story of perseverance—everything is a matter of perspective.

Murphy had seemed very attractive in his photos, which is why I'd swiped right, but meeting in person was still a welcome surprise. He was taller than I'd expected, easily over 200lbs. of solid muscle, and had a beautiful smile of perfectly straight white teeth—not to mention he asked me questions about myself non-stop (a rarity on a first date to be honest). When we hugged hello, I breathed in the thick scent of cologne and body odor, which sounds gross but was deeply alluring. His pheromones had me wrapped around their little finger. When he asked if I wanted to come back to his hotel room I practically jumped into his arms, which honestly looked like they could carry all 300 pounds of me without breaking a sweat. I agreed to go back to his hotel room but the whole walk there (you know, across the street), I was nervous about the bomb I'd have to drop on him—I was bleeding like a tsunami.

If you're asking why I even bothered to get dressed for a first date when my uterus was looking like that elevator scene in the Shining, I would say because he was only in town for one night and he was on the Olympic Jamaican bobsled team like you don't think there was going to at least be a story worth retelling in the mix?

And if you're thinking, why did I agree to go back to his hotel when my pristine-vagine was currently being plugged by a tampon channeling the strength of the hoover dam, the answer is because I wasn't about to miss out on at least a hot make out with an elite athlete. What can I say, I like to be a champion by proxy or whatever? Murphy was smoking hot and built like a brick house, and I'd spent my whole life going on dates and avoiding fucking while on my period. Seven out of every twenty-eight days is a lot of your life to spend hiding away and not living up to the potential fun I deserved. The amount of time I'd already wasted because of an inconvenient monthly flow seemed astronomical. Goddamn it, I deserved this.

People don't talk enough about periods—that's just a fact (and changing that fact is the hill I'm willing to die on). I would be forty before anyone ever asked if my periods were notably heavy in a way that I could answer yeah you know I think they might be.

Back in grad school, my doctor had asked me how many cups of coffee I drink a day. I lied, obviously, and divided the truth in half which seemed reasonable—"Five cups," I said. She gasped, which should've been a clue right there but either because I lied or because we simply hadn't put two and two together yet, it went no further.

I've been anemic since I was thirteen, and if I'm being honest, pretty goddamn tired ever since. Doctors had noticed my anemia, but no one seemed especially concerned by it. "We'll just keep an eye on it," they'd say and stress that I should find some ways to get more iron in my diet or take a supplement. I tried several supplements, none of which made a difference except hurting my stomach, so I stopped bothering.

That day, after the question about coffee, my doctor suggested I try to have no more than one cup of coffee a day, and all I could think was, "Are you insane?" Some days, by dinnertime, I'm so exhausted it feels like I'm too tired to breathe so yeah, I'll put the coffee cup down once we get some goddamn iron in these veins and I stop bleeding like a broken dam once a month.

That won't happen for another few years (closer to six than two) when I get an IUD to stop my periods. The iron infusions I'd gotten before my IUD had done nothing but once my periods stopped and I started back on a regular iron supplement. Within months my anemia was gone and when I tell you the change to my energy levels has been night and day (day being a thing I'm excited and awake enough to enjoy because for the first time in thirty years I'm no longer bleeding to death every month).

But we're here now, in this story, where I'm thirty-three and every period has me bleeding like when they bring out "Can Nachos" and lift the can up and all the nachos come pouring out uncontrollably. Something like that.

Murphy and I were already kissing by the time the elevator doors shut. Inside the hotel room, I quickly blurted out that this was lovely and everything but that I had my period, and it was heavy so we couldn't fuck. The man was not fazed. Clothes were removed, tampons were unplugged (by me, in the bathroom, when ready, I mean I'm not a psychopath), and a towel was put spread out on the bed.

And just like Moses, that man parted the red sea.

Did I feel bad for the murder scene we caused all over the hotel sheets? Ab-so-fucking-lutely. Would I do it again given the choice? In an Olympic minute.

Not really one to enjoy sleeping over, I left him later that evening. He moved to the other bed in the room (the one not an active crime scene) and I waved goodbye as strutted out the door. Upon returning home, a quick google told me everything he'd said about himself had been true with the exception of being single, that was up for debate. If only John Candy could see me now.

A TALE OF THREE ANDY'S

If I had to choose one word to describe the entirety of my dating life, it would be mediocrity. Mediocre men. Mediocre expectations. Mediocre interest. Of this, I am certain. Where things get hazy is how exactly I got here.

That's a lie. I know exactly how I got here. It was fatphobia all along.

From a very young age, I've known that the world hates fat people. I've heard all the bullshit about how men will fuck a fat girl but not date her, how they love to get head from a fat girl because of something Drake (and all the pathetic men before him) said, how fat women are simultaneously hyper sexualized and de-sexualized in nearly equal measure. I know all about the self-hatred of the men who love (the bodies) fat women. I've always known that they were the weak ones, the fucked-up ones, even if they were the majority, even if it was their world that I had to live in.

But I also know about the men who love (like really love) fat women. Who aren't afraid to claim us, who look deep into our eyes just to tell us how beautiful we are, who see us as more than a body—to those men we are people with personalities and feelings—whole, complete, precious.

So, while I know there are the men who hate us (and the men who hate themselves for loving us), and there are the men who simply don't check for us, there are also the men who cherish us. That's why I keep dating. That's why I kept dating and wading my way through the mediocrity. And also, why I sometimes accepted the mediocrity. Because I was passing the time. Because every so often you'd run into a really great guy, or a really great story, that made all the mediocrity worth it.

I didn't accept less because I deserved less. I accepted less because that was what was available to me. As a fat woman, living in a wildly fatphobic (read: thin and materialistic) city like Vancouver, my options were limited. It was that simple.

Whenever I talk with other non-fat women about dating, the discussion is always about finding this one great love, a partner, a companion, while I've spent most of my dating life just trying to be seen as a person, respected as a complex human being. Why was it so hard for men to value me (when I knew I had so much value on offer)? I wasn't desperate to be loved by men, but I was certainly desperate to understand them. Even now, I'm still waiting to meet even one man eloquent enough to explain himself to me. Dating, and the behaviour of men, was full of riddles I couldn't unravel (but that doesn't mean I wouldn't still try).

Andy #1 was a nightmare from the start. The first time he messaged was on plenty of fish sometime back around 2011. He had made me laugh with his messages (a rarity), so when I googled him and found an article online about how he'd been involved in some sort of cocaine scandal causing him to lose his job as a firefighter, I ignored it. We all have a past, right? He was now working for the city in a slightly different capacity. It's truly amazing the way white men can bounce back from anything (and continue to prosper).

Aside from general white-man-success, Andy also had charm going for him. When he suggested a phone call before meeting, I (privately) sulked. I hate talking on the phone—I'm a millennial in all the worst ways (don't you ever show up to my house without texting first). Even though I was already sweating through my shirt, I agreed, and we ended up talking on the phone for two hours. Laughing, banter, we had it all. By the time the call was over, Andy had charmed my pants off (metaphorically speaking).

Unfortunately, as excited as I had been to go out with him, I was just as quickly disappointed by his inability to make it happen. We made plans twice (which is one time too many). When Andy flaked for the second time, regardless of his excuse being that he got called into work, I was done (or was I?).

The thing about mediocrity in dating is that it will regularly make you question the reality of what is and isn't *terrible* dating behavior. I'll end something with a man, even a man I've never met, over the feeling that my time is being wasted. If I'm being honest, it's a friendship dealbreaker for me to. But because the world is filled with so many actual terrible things (like war and violence), there are times I've given men too many graces because I didn't want to be a bitch. I didn't want to be seen as a bitch. I wasn't sure if maybe I actually *was* a bitch. If I've learned anything about myself during these last ten years of dating, it's this—I no longer care if anyone thinks I'm a bitch—in fact, I almost prefer it. But that's now, and we must go back to then.

    The fear of being a bitch is arguably the most logical reason that I settled for mediocrity in dating. I never settled out of the fear of not finding love (I already loved myself enough). Plus, I never really understood the idea of putting up with terrible treatment out of the fear that this was as good as it could get because the truth is that being alone would always be better than being hurt by someone I cared for (and especially someone I didn't). Men (outside of my father) really didn't add much to my life—the idea that I'd settle for one of them mistreating me in order to have someone to watch tv with at night was absolutely fucking bonkers. And look, I get it, I get the urge to have a partner and/or a family, to have a place to call home, a place to feel safe and connected and loved, but men who treat you badly aren't providing that. It's like settling for a thing that's only in your imagination. But again, lest you think I'm being judgmental and dishonest, I want to be as clear as fucking day—I was a settler. Whether it was the fear of being a bitch or just an undeniable boredom and naïve belief that there was fun I could potentially be missing out on, I regularly gave men *undeserved* first and second (and even third) chances.

    The difference between a deserved and undeserved second chance is all in how someone attempts to make up for disappointing you. For example, if you have to cancel plans with someone, contact them immediately. Do not wait for them to check in with you to see if plans are still on (they're not, right? So fucking cancel already what's your fucking problem, Andy). Be apologetic and be sincere about it and if you want to see them again, reschedule deliberately and immediately. Some people are just assholes who are cavalier about wasting the time of others and so if someone cancels on you and doesn't apologize, and doesn't attempt to reschedule, delete them off your roster immediately. Sure, they might come back another time and ask you out again but it's too late now, you've seen who they are. Please, for the love of God, learn from this mistake I make over and over and over again in dating by trying to be understanding and nice. Some people will simply waste your time (because they don't respect you) and never give it a second thought. It's rude as fuck and they should be shot immediately for doing so. Or [insert something a chill, non-bitch would say].

Not all lessons can be learned overnight though, so after the first time Andy cancelled, I didn't delete his number (which was stupid but understandable). The second time Andy cancelled; I deleted his number immediately. I felt like a real bad bitch (in the best sense). I forgot about Andy almost immediately.

Years went by, I moved, I moved again, I moved back, and then there was Andy in my inbox messaging me on Plenty of Fish like this was our first interaction. I didn't waver. I quickly reminded him that he'd had his shot and blew it (hell yeah!) but after profusely apologizing and assuring me he'd changed jobs and was no longer working on-call, I agreed to one final chance (like a fucking idiot).

This time, though, Andy #1 did not cancel, and we went for a walk on the pier. Normally, I hate walking dates, and I hate dates where a man doesn't have to buy me something (if you're not going into debt for me what is even the fucking point?). But given Andy's track record, I wasn't about to put up with any nonsense. He was getting a half hour and I was going to be wearing jeans and a hoodie. The conversation was good and somewhere on the pier he kissed me, and I let him because I'm a slut who loves a good kiss. He said he just had to, said he wanted to see if there was a connection.

"There is," he said with my lipgloss on his lips.

Driving home I couldn't help but wonder if I had been wrong about second chances (or third chances as was the case with Andy #1) all along?

On our second date, I drove over to his place. I thought we were going to watch a movie but instead we watched some UFC bullshit. He fed me baby carrots in the kitchen because I was absolutely starving but that's all I "wanted" (and we both just stood there pretending my internalized fatphobia wasn't a thing). Andy #1's biggest redeeming quality was that he repeatedly tried to make me something more substantial for dinner. Though I turned him down, I found the gesture wildly endearing (which is probably why I let him kiss me on the couch). And why, after kissing on the couch for a while, I let him take me upstairs and kiss in his bed. And the gesture was probably why, though I wasn't going to fuck Andy that night, I gave him a handjob. I gave him a handjob because he'd tried to make me eat a full dinner, he wanted me to be eating enough (something almost no man had ever done before). I have him a handjob because I was good at gibing them, and it fed my ego watching how easily I could get him off. I gave him a handjob because I thought there'd be a third and fourth date. I gave him a handjob because—and I can't stress this enough—I still hadn't learned to read or understand men.

I thought there'd be fun and fucking but there was neither. Andy texted again but never made plans, not really and not fast enough and never with enough enthusiasm. Maybe some people wanted to casually hang out once every few weeks, when their schedules allowed, but I was trying to form a connection and if I'm being honest, without decently regular and interesting conversation or interaction, it was hard to sustain an interest in most of the men I dated. Andy was no aberration. In our final text exchange, Andy assured me he was interested but busy and I assured him I was uninterested in busy men. Men are never that busy. Their busyness is always a lie.

Between the first and second date with Andy #1, I went on a date with Andy #2. The date was weird to say the least (but when have I ever said the least!). He chose this restaurant that ended up being attached to a hotel, but not like a fancy or funky hotel—a nearly suburban hotel. The restaurant, which we didn't need since we were just going for drinks, was so empty you could hear a shoe squeak and so well-lit I wanted to wear sunglasses (I didn't because I'm not a psycho, but you get the drift). Somewhere between laughing at how awkward and weird this place was and having banter, we fell in love.

I'm joking of course.

Just once I want there to be a need to write out the dialogue exactly as it happened because we were both so hilarious and interesting the page necessitates it. Which isn't to say that the banter was bad. It was good enough. He asked lots of questions (as did I) and the conversation flowed as it does. He was a film producer (in about the same way that I'm a writer). We were both trying. We were artists getting by. We were creatives with dreams. Two hours had passed, and we were the only people left in the restaurant.

While walking to my car a few blocks from the restaurant, we stopped at an intersection to let a car pass. He pulled me close and kissed me. As someone who avoids PDA like the plague, I'm not a fan of the public first kiss. But his lips were pillowy soft and matched perfectly with my rhythm and just like that we were two full-grown adults kissing on a street corner. Luckily, the street corner knew how to dim its lights (a lesson that restaurant could learn).

Men regularly tell me that I'm a great kisser, so much so that I assume they say it to all the women they kiss every time they kiss them. I've never thought that much of it except to note that I rarely return the compliment because I'm an honest bitch and I don't give compliments I don't mean (handjobs, sure, but never compliments). When Andy #2 kissed me on that street corner, I melted (purely from the physicality of it all). Andy was a nice enough guy, but I was by no means swooning over him, that is until he kissed me with those delicious lips and perfect technique. He was a great kisser.

I hadn't been planning to go home with him. Not before our date, not during our date, and even as he walked me to my car, I had zero intention of continuing on back to his place. But his kisses had put a spell on me and before I could act more rationally, we were meeting back at his place. Inside his west end apartment, we sat on his loveseat and smoked weed and watched a funny movie and it was fine. It was fun. *It was fine*. It's hard to write about these men and these ordinary dates from my place in the future where I know far better. But in the moment, the date did exactly what I wanted it to do (until it didn't).

That night back at Andy #2's apartment, after the joint and the movie and during the making out, he fingered me, sort of. Andy fingered me with the lack of aptitude and skill that you'd expect from a first timer or a man in his early twenties (and Andy #2 was cusping around 30). Andy lamely fingered me, and I sucked his dick like I was defending a title and it was fun, it was fine. It was to be expected. That night, I went home smiling, and when he asked me to hang out again, I said yes.

I was absolutely excited about it (because I didn't know better). But I need you to know that the woman writing this story knows better, knows that there *is better*, knows that I was biding my time back then. I need you to know that I knew what I was getting myself into (mostly) and that I knew what I was settling for (mostly), and I was fine to do that because I was bored. I say mostly because I find that settling for men is a bit like quicksand—you think you're settling for casual sex and orgasms but more often than not the sex you think is what you're "settling" for is actually pretty unsatisfying and you're fucking around with a man who doesn't care whether or not you'll have an orgasm. But you don't know that part in the moment.

I didn't want a relationship, but I did want to cum. So, while I need you to know that I knew what I was doing (in that Andy #2 was just a bit of fun, and I had zero expectations outside of that), I still didn't know that a man who fingered like a teenage virgin would also fuck like one. I knew it was lame that he fingered me (unsatisfactorily), and I gave him a (phenomenal) beej, but I hadn't yet learned to stop temporarily rewarding men in the hopes that the next time would be better. Please know that I know better now; that I would never, could never now. But this is now and that was then.

Back then, I thought men didn't go down on me because I was fat. I thought that they weren't good at fingering me because I was fat, and they struggled to understand my fupa, my apron belly, or any of the most basic characteristics of fat female anatomy. My god, the weight I used to put on my fatness.

It should've occurred to me to ask them. It should've occurred to me to insist (in a consensual way) on reciprocity. I guess, in some fucked up way, it did occur to me, but because of all the years I'd spent being pressured into giving a man more than I wanted, it irked me that I had to ask. Plus, if I'm being really *really* fucking real—I also wasn't asking because of my own anti-fatness (and awareness of its proliferation in our society), because there was some small part of me that felt like maybe I was gross for the way my body decided to fold and exist. Just because I was long past the days when the fatphobic words of men could hurt me, didn't mean I wanted to risk experiencing those words in person. Not that I hadn't had men lovingly and passionately eat my pussy till I came moaning and screaming but that was what relationship pleasure was like and this was casual. There was another layer to it as well. I didn't want a man to lick my pussy, to make me cum, because I'd asked him to, and he'd acquiesced. If he wasn't drooling for it, if he wasn't absolutely falling all over himself just to get his mouth on my pussy as fast as possible, then I didn't really want him to. Then, of course, I didn't really want him, but if I never asked, I'd never have to know.

How completely fucked up it was that men were always getting pleasure, and I was not? While not lost on me, it wasn't as glaring and obvious to me then as it is now. Back then I had a clue but still hadn't really put the puzzle pieces together. It always felt like I was some kind of let down because I rarely came from sex and that was just somehow my burden to bear alone. My god, the bullshit we teach young women and believe about ourselves until we know better).

The night of our second date, a term I use loosely since it was really just a hookup (and that was fine with both of us), we watched *Lock, Stock, and Two Smoking Barrels*, which as a filmmaker he should've known was a real weird choice for a date when you're trying to get in the mood. But when you're horny, you're horny, so with a little weed and a few kisses, we were back and over the couch to his probably-normal-sized bed (though it absolutely seemed smaller than a queen sized) pushed right up against his mirrored closets.

As he was sliding his dick inside me way too early, he kept saying, "We have to be quiet because my neighbor is this really old lady who always complains," and I couldn't help thinking, *who on earth would be making noise from this level of fucking?* Because it certainly wasn't going to be me. While the kissing had been svelte perfection, Andy #2's fucking was awkward and off-beat.

We were both in our thirties, so I could hardly believe how bad the sex was—aren't you supposed to have picked up a few clues along the way? Then again, remembering his fingering abilities made it all make sense. As it turns out, his kissing was an aberration he couldn't live up to. His mouth was writing checks his dick couldn't cash. Honestly, he fucked like how I imagine a virgin fucks with their mom watching tv in the other room. After he came, I went to the bathroom to pee and mime a few *what the actual fuck*s at myself in the mirror while trying to keep my laughter from bubbling up.

I drove home trying to convince myself that it hadn't been that bad (which by the way is an absolute bullshit thing women do that needs to stop immediately). The way I/we excuse the fixable inadequacies men and give these endless chances in the hopes that a man will improve himself is beyond ridiculous and definitely an undeserved grace.

Was it because I was fat? Everything always comes back to fatness.

I used to think that fatness was why I was always settling, but I've learned that thin women settle all the time. Conventionally attractive women settle all the time. None of us are being treated how we deserve. And while I would never, ever, not ever, not even for a fucking second suggest someone should reward this kind of unsatisfying sex and overall treatment from a man they actually like, there was still one truly lame reason of my own that I was settling for Andy #2 (aside from the fact that his middle name was Juan which allowed me to call him *Andy #2 - Juan that I Juanted* as a way to differentiate him from Andy #1). As much as it's difficult to admit, his reward (of sex with me) seemed inconsequential to fulfilling my need to not be bored. But that's because it hadn't really occurred to me that someone could be cumming from casual sex. It didn't even really seem like an option let alone something that would be expected. The bar is truly in hell.

Men think they have this monopoly on dating and hooking up with people they deem beneath them because of boredom but let me assure you, boredom has absolutely been the biggest motivator throughout my entire dating life. Anytime I've ever settled, it's been out of boredom. I knew I deserved far more than Andy #2 (and Andy #1) would ever have to offer. It wasn't about insecurity or not believing my own worth, it was a matter of opportunity and impatience. That said, I wasn't getting orgasms like all the Andy's in my life were and looking back that seems far more devastating and pathetic than it did at the time, but we all have a journey, and I guess cumming is mine.

By the time I go out with Andy #3, I start to worry about the creativity of our parents' generation and the malleability of my attraction. Why were there so many of them, these boys named Andy who didn't appreciate me the way I wanted them to. I start to worry my type is stupidity (theirs and mine).

    I go out with Andy #3 three times (which feels like a math problem but is just the truth). I go out with Andy on three totally separate occasions and in three totally separate headspaces. Andy never changes, not once. Andy #3 is himself the whole way through; I am progressively losing my mind.

    For weeks Andy messaged and texted me every single day. Every. Single. Fucking. Day. Several times a day. When I didn't respond fast enough to his texts, he would message again and again on Tinder.

> *Are you getting my messages?*
> *How was your day?*
> *Send me a picture?*
> *Tell me what you're up to.*

Before we ever meet, Andy #3 is so fucking curious, a thing I desperately want from men, but his impatience for my response is an irritant. Now, two days after we've met and had a fantastic first date, now he's nonchalant. Now he's in no rush. Now he's no longer so fucking curious.

Andy tracks the paths of ground water. He calculates to figure out where the water running under a proposed mine site will end up. "It's mostly calculus," he explains.

Why can't he do the calculus on this? Why doesn't he know how this nonchalance, this casual and abrupt lack of enthusiasm, will dilute my excitement? Why can't he see the spillage, the exact place where the flood will happen.

For weeks before meeting, Andy had messaged multiple times a day, and now that we'd met and were no longer so far apart, the dam of my desire was breaking in his silence. My interest had burst and was running dry, all because he changed the pace of contact. Andy had set a precedent of texting every single morning, every day and now that there was nothing from him, there would be nothing between us.

I have lost my mind in the time it takes to…text a woman back.

I am the worst version of myself after a first date. In the silence (and uncertainty) following a first date, I'm creating data reports in my mind. Mapping out a hypothetical chart for the timing of text messages. Who messaged first each day? (Him). How long did it take between responses? (Varied). When did I become so pathetic? (unknowable). Why can't I stop freaking out? (To be determined). Do I even like him? (What does that matter?)

The irony is that all the texting and attention before meeting was a burden, an inconvenience, just another example of a man imposing himself onto my time before there was anything real between us. I didn't know him before. He was just a stranger on Tinder who had "super liked" me, which could be an indication of intense interest or just sloppy fingers—you can't trust anything on the apps. Men are always putting in effort and interest at the wrong times. Too much in the beginning, too little after we've met.

When we matched on tinder, he messaged right away. I didn't respond immediately, but he just kept messaging. By the time he asked me out and my interest had been piqued enough to say yes, a week and a half in, he was in the Yukon for three weeks working.

I'm so excited to see you he typed.

Sorry, I wrote, *you should've told me earlier that you were going to be away for three weeks.* I wasn't really sorry though; men were always rushing me. Him being away gave us the space to get to know each other.

Sorry, he typed, *I wasn't sure if you were interested.* He was right to be unsure. I wasn't sure I was interested either. But he kept asking me questions, in addition to the usual *you're so hot* chatter. Men (who are attracted to me) are always telling me how attracted to me they are. As if I didn't know. As if I didn't understand what swiping right and having full blown conversations meant. As if it would endear me to them, but I knew I was hot, and the compliment (especially before meeting) was virtually worthless. Attraction is a fickle business. Men cannot be trusted to always want to fuck you. A man will think you're so hot he could die one day and the forget your name the next.

Every day Andy texted about how excited he was to meet me. He sent pictures I hadn't asked to see (such a turnoff), and then pictures I had asked for (snow covered forests of the Yukon so brilliant they solved math problems). Half his steps were wrong, but the right ones made up for the ground lost (because men always get the benefit of the doubt). And then one day I asked him to resend a picture, *this time a little lower down*. If I was going to be bombarded with shirtless poorly lit pics, I might as well get a glimpse of something more interesting. Because now there was a possibility, I'd see it in person. Because now it was a preview rather than unaware bragging. Men have such little concept of the value of their dicks (babe, they're worthless). He acquiesced almost before I typed the request and then lamented having to wait to see me.

By the time he was back in town, our timing was off again. I had pulled a muscle in my neck and managed to catch a cold, and then it was the Christmas holidays. He was in Maine (or New Hampshire or Vermont or Connecticut—one of those white boy/rich family states) for the holiday. By the time we finally met, we had been talking for over a month. He wasn't nervous at all; I was terribly so.

He'd told me how excited he was to meet so many *many* times that I started to fear I could never live up to whatever he had imagined me to be. How could anyone? Then again, he had already seen me in pictures with my hair up and fresh faced. I hadn't wanted him to see me without my hair and makeup done; that was the Achilles heel of my last remaining (jk) insecurities. But he had asked and asked, and I had felt pressured so I told him that he should respect my answer (read: fuck off). I told him he should respect my desire not to send a fresh-faced pic simply because he had said *I like girls with their hair up, I'm sure you look great, I just want to see you right now.* I told him that *maybe we could both live in a world where men respect what I say the first time instead of pressuring me to acquiesce to whatever their current desire of me was.* He apologized-ish and said he *hadn't meant to pressure me*, but then again men never seem to mean the pressure every time they try to navigate around a woman's boundaries.

A few days later, after the feeling of pressure had worn off, I thought fuck it. I was so tired of feeling like I had to be my absolute goddamn prettiest self in front of men. I was tired of always having to wear a shield; dating wasn't supposed to be a battle, was it? I wanted to show him who he was really getting right from the beginning, and if he didn't like it, then that would be that, and at least then I'd have more time on my hands. If he didn't think I was beautiful without any guards up, at least I wouldn't have to go on another first date (that would most certainly end in disaster).

But he loved it.

Over the next few days, I sent him several more just-as-I-am photos and every time he responded with tremendous excitement, his excitement became our excitement. Finally, I agreed to meet.

The night of our first date, I waited outside the bar wearing a denim jacket (adorable) and a down jacket bejeweled with 'Apple Bottoms' branding across the back (because it was absolutely freezing, and Apple Bottoms was in style the last time it was this cold in Vancouver). He rode his bike, which seemed ridiculous because of the cold and good-for-him because of climate change. When we leaned in to hug each other, I realized I had completely forgotten to ask how tall he was and instead imagined it based on how I thought he looked in his pictures. I had thought he was going to be 6'2" and he was more like 5'10" which is fine except for the difference in my imagination. I couldn't help but wonder if I, too, was already a disappointment to him.

In the immediate aftermath of a first date, I have a habit of thinking it went better than it did, that he was more impressive than he was. I think it's all the pheromones or just the leaning in of trying to have a good attitude or the having to hype everything up inside my own brain because men are such a fucking snooze that if I didn't, I'd never go on another first date again and life is long and there are just so many nights to fill. Plus, I love adventure. Some people like to climb mountains and I just wanted to climb some dick.

Except not really. I just wanted a man to make me laugh and turn me on (enough to want to climb his dick). Often when I look back on dates, I wonder how much of it was hype and how much of it was real. It usually takes years (and further interactions) to realize how much of my own happiness is dealt by my own hand. Which is either incredibly sad or unbelievably wonderful depending on how you look at it. They are rarely the Ace of Spades I feel them to be.

The date with Andy #3 had been good enough, there was cute and fun conversation at the restaurant over a delicious snack of spinach and artichoke dip. I love a date with food—another thing I was desperately tired of was diet culture and how it affected my ability to just have a good time. I would no longer tell men I wasn't hungry. He drank a little but not too much and I sipped my soda like the delightful angel I am. When the bill came, he paid—as he *fucking* should, and when we left, he asked if I wanted to go back to his place.

Men paying on first dates is the hill I will die on. *Aren't you a Feminist?* Yes, I'm a Feminist and it's the very reason I think this way. Men risk nothing on a first date. Women risk everything. Until there's no wage gap and no orgasm gap and women can safely run at night with headphones in and everyone believes women and sexual assault is always taken seriously and men don't murder women at alarming rates—then we can talk about women paying for their half on a first date. Until then, I'm dead on this hill. No caveats. No questions.

Walking into Andy's apartment, all I could think about was how unfair it was that men had so many ways (other than just being hot) to attract a woman (when women really just have "being hot"). Andy's apartment was on Oak Street near Broadway in Vancouver, which I only mention for context because it's one of the most expensive cities to live in, and while his kitchen was small, he had a 3rd floor apartment with a large bedroom, normal sized bathroom, and *huge* living room. So huge, in fact, that he had a full-on L-shaped couch, 8-person dining table with benches on either side, multiple small tables and other expected furniture and still enough spare room to do a full dance routine.

Perhaps I really should've gotten a degree in the sciences because damn, those boys were getting paid.

A good apartment can really make you want to fuck. Maybe not entirely, not from scratch, but if the date hasn't been fireworks, and his height is a small disappointment and the way he sort-of a had a squeaky voice is a turn off—his huge (and adult decorated) apartment will be a turn-right-back-on. All I had to impress men were my tits (and double-d personality). If I was trying to fuck his apartment, I would've stripped right there beside the coffee table.

The drinks he'd poured for us were barely on the coffee table when he kissed me. Moments before, I had been thinking that this date wasn't even that great, that maybe I'd never have a really great first date, when suddenly the earth was shaking. Our lips were pressed together and while my heart wasn't exactly in it, my loins definitely were, and just like that our bodies were swaying with the movements of the earth. My opinion of hooking up with him, like a tectonic plate, had shifted, but that's because, of course, literal tectonic plates had shifted. As it turned out, while mid-kiss, we experienced an earthquake, literally. Twenty minutes later and people we're already tweeting about it. That's the thing about magic, or a total coincidence of nature, but something happens when you're feeling moderate to good about a man and then (through no skill of his own) something straight out of a romcom occurs. The earth shifted and Andy got in just a little.

And by got in, I mean to my heart and my mouth. Yes, dear reader, I sucked this man's dick and I'm here to tell you my performance was flawless (and his pleasure undeserved) as always. That's the thing about earthquakes, they can really shake you up in best/worst ways.

The next day, I hoped Andy would text. He did not. Then, another day came and went, and Andy still didn't text. This man who had pestered me all day long before he knew anything real about me was now devastatingly silent, and I was filled with an unwarranted rage. There is no way all this rage is about him—of that I was unmistakably aware. I knew I was being irrational and an asshole, but I couldn't seem to stop myself from hating that things couldn't go smoothly just once. Just one fucking time.

It will seem bonkers to have the level of certainty I had that he would eventually ask me out again. That's the thing about dating men, well, my experience in dating men. They always liked me somewhat. Of that I was certain. The rage (which was really just frustration) that ignited inside me wasn't about rejection—it was about the soft nonchalance they always seemed to have. The gentle way they couldn't get it up for me in any way I valued. There dicks were always as hard as their schedules were to fit me into. I couldn't tell if it was the men I was picking, or it was something I was giving off.

What do you mean sucking the dick of a loser who has done nothing to deserve it gives the wrong idea?

I knew he'd ask me out again. He'd arrive in my messages like a lost package tossed carelessly on my doorstep. He'd show up again and ask me out in a few weeks was my best guess—that's what I'd tell people—at the gym, my friends, anyone who was gracious enough not to judge me for the terrible way I was behaving, for the way I couldn't seem to reign it in.

"Long after my enthusiasm for him has wilted," I say, "he'll ask me out again, and it'll be too late." I make elaborate gestures of closing windows and shutting doors. It's all so very dramatic. But it doesn't take weeks, it takes days.

He types: *What are you up to?*

He types: *When are we getting together again?*

Five days after our first date, he texted as if he hadn't gone through the same days of silence that I had (after all the weeks of constant messaging). Five days of silence with someone you've yet to meet is nothing. Five days after a first date without any contact, is an eternity. I had already gone from thinking that my enthusiasm would wain to its actual waning. I was no longer sure I wanted to see him again. Sorry, what I really mean to say is that I was sure I no longer wanted to see him again. Not really, and not like how I did before.

I type: *Just about to go to a coffee shop and do some writing* but it feels too harsh to leave his question unanswered, so I add: *Idk, when we're you thinking?* I no longer know why I bother. I don't correct my grammar typo. Every message is a bother.

Oh nice. Maybe tomorrow or Monday or any other day next week.

I couldn't meet up with him tomorrow even if I had wanted to (I didn't want to) because I was going down to Seattle to "see a friend." That's what I'd say if he asked, but the truth was I was going to see my ex.

Yes, we still loved each other. Yes, we fucked when we were together, but we were rarely together. He lived in another city. I was living my life. It was all very entangled and uncomplicated at the same time, which doesn't make sense but love never does.

The text message from Andy sat unanswered while I sat in Starbucks sulking because I had wanted this one time to be easy. Why couldn't it ever be fucking easy? I knew I was being a baby, but I didn't care. He'd waited too long to text me after our first date and he'd missed asking me out for a Saturday night, and I was offended on both accounts.

I was going away tomorrow, and I wanted to be going away forever. I wanted to write *I'm leaving town tomorrow, I'm leaving for good, you missed your chance*. Like I was some kind of priceless artifact, a unicorn of fantastical proportions. I just wanted one guy, one time, to see me right away and decide that I was who he wanted. Not forever, not only and always, just right now, for sure, definitely, no question. I wanted a man who was certain.

But Andy was human, and he had wobbled. And I had waned. And now here we were. With a text message (far beyond the one I thought would be the last) not knowing how to respond, sulking in a Starbucks, trying to write about something other than sex and dating.

"Why don't you write about murder or radiation poisoning," my mother says.

"You just like those stories because they're not real for you. They're all things you never have to worry about."

"Is that why?" she asks.

"Yes." I say, "You don't like what I write because it's real, it's happening. You don't want to know that men are monsters." And then we have a discussion where I have to, again, explain the difference between fiction and non-fiction, and our privileged lives, and by the end I've devolved into a rant about how I will always protect women over men and she says, "You sound like a man hater," and I say, "I am," and more than partly mean it.

Andy is not a monster, he is a time waster, a frustrater, an irritant. I respond to Andy and tell him that I'm free on Wednesday night if he wants to hang out. I think about saying Tuesday. I think about how many nights I will spend in Seattle. I don't want to be rushed if I want to stay an extra night. I don't want to be rushed because I'm not even sure if I want to see Andy #3 anymore. Those five days of silence after making out during an earthquake had taken a toll on my interest. He had fucking ruined it. They were always fucking ruining it. I had already changed his name in my phone. He'd gone from Andrew Tinder to Andy #3. He was just another Andy now, just another disappointment. My mother would say that I'm too hard on men, but I would argue that I was always too easy.

He says: *Haha. You are busy until then ;-)* and doesn't use any punctuation except a fucking winky face. I don't know if this is a question I'm supposed to answer or just an off-the-cuff remark about the fact that I've chosen a day midweek, which seems greedy for a man who had already missed two opportunities to lock down a second date. Two opportunities or a thousand—what did any of it even matter? He wasn't at all worried that I would just float on out of his life.

Everyone says I'm so brave the way I put myself out there, the way I go on dates and take rejection and risk these feelings. But I have to wonder how often I cause my own misery. How often I find a way to end things before they can be ended on me (but if the ending is a constant—what does it matter who ends it anyway?). God, I was so bored of not being chosen. That's not really the whole truth though because fuck the idea of being *chosen* and also, I had been chosen before, just not recently, just not often enough to keep it lodged in my memory. I wanted a man to put his nonchalance on the shelf and say *that girl! That girl right there! She seems amazing!* And to do it on the back of a first date, on the shoulders of actual experience not prior to meeting. I wanted a man to display a level of excitement and certainty when it mattered because it was based on something real and not on the bullshit connection of texting and imaginations and hope. Their excitement before we meet is always bullshit.

Andy had said *Maybe tomorrow or Monday or any other day next week* about us going out again and I responded with the truth.

I said: *I'm going to Seattle and I'm not sure when I'm coming back.*

He said: *Awesome*

and then typed and deleted something.

I said: *Haha sorry that sounded really cryptic…I'm not sure if I'm coming back Monday or Tuesday.*

He said: *What are you doing down there*

I said: *Going to visit a friend*

He said: *Awesome*

And we were right back to where we were before the conversation ever started. No plans had been made. No second date was on the books. Wobble and wane.

Unsurprisingly, Wednesday with Andy never happens. We left our last conversation with no conclusion except to say that Wednesday was when I was free. He made no plans. He made no moves.

While I'm in Seattle, Andy texts to ask if I'm having fun and I respond that I am. On my drive home from Seattle, the day of the evening we're supposed to go out, Andy texts to say that he's swamped with work stuff and has to cancel. He doesn't suggest rescheduling. I change his name in my phone to YOU DESERVE BETTER. Throughout the weekend and then the following week, Andy continues to text but never makes anything happen. It's a lot of *how's your day going* and zero date scheduling. Andy uses a lot of words and says nothing.

On the following Monday, he asks about my weekend. His turtle pace rubs me the wrong way like knees sliding across carpet. His compliments land worthlessly at my feet.

I respond: so, *what's up?* By which I mean WHAT THE FUCK DO YOU WANT?!? but he takes to mean, *what are you up to right now?* and proceeds to tell me.

He texts: *just relaxing on the couch*

The man is truly a thrill ride.

I ask if the only reason he'd texted was to find out about my weekend. He said that it was: *And also to try and make plans*, which was exactly what I wanted him to say so that I could say the thing I'd been dying to say for two weeks now.

I tell him that what he has on offer is not enough. I tell him that his mediocre interest is not something I'm interested in. Andy tells me that his interest is not mediocre. I tell him that the time for romance between us has passed (and then before I can stop myself) I offer friendship as a consolation prize. He said it's a bummer, but he understands.

I'm immediately filled with regret for selling my friendship so short. It's too late though, the words have already spilled out, the offer has been made.

Andy types an explanation I hadn't asked for: *I know I have been distant and not connecting.*

Now, purely out of curiosity, I am asking: *Any particular reason?*

No not really. Just skiing most weekends. And not really taking the time to see how you have been and what is new and make plans for us.

He was confessing to scheduling issues or pointing out some incumbrances that simply couldn't be gotten over, but all I heard was him admitting he wasn't interested enough. I can't stand the way men mince words and waste your time. Sometimes I think maybe they don't even know what they're feeling themselves. It was hard to hear (through his turtle-paced explanations) that he just didn't like me enough. But I'll be honest in that I'm both experienced in being rejected and also find it not that big of a deal. Sure, I might have a little cry or tantrum. The disappointment will take a few days to seep out through my pores. But surely, by the end of the week, two at the most, I'll be over it. I'll have perspective. I won't be worried about him anymore.

Andy wasn't interested enough, but he was still interested. The truth is he wasn't worried about putting in the work because he'd figured I'd be waiting around for him when he finally got to it. Andy was wrong, of course. But it didn't matter much either way—my interest was scrapped. Both Andy and my interest—straight in the bin.

As if offering friendship wasn't a mistake to begin with, in the awkward silence I doubled down on the thing I hadn't even really wanted to offer in the first place. *Okay, well like I said if you want to be friends we can hang out (though if you weren't that motivated to hang out before, not sure how much you'd be now lol)* and then I ended it with a wink so it would seem bitchy but like, in a cute way.

He said he thought it was clever and I said: *Always.*

I like that about u.

Which I already knew.

I knew he liked me, moderately, somewhat, more than neutral, just not enough. I said something cute, he laughed, it was a real chuckle fest (which I then felt the need to crush in order to solidify the nothingness between us). Even in friendship, I wanted things to be clear. Plus, after I no longer liked someone, I'd say anything. You can be as open and vulnerable (and bitchy and rigid) as you want once you don't care if that person wants to kiss you anymore. I said: *All this said though, I have to tell you, I'm not a huge fan of uncertainty (I like to know where I stand with people, who wants to spend time wondering what's up when that time could be spent having fun) so if you're smarting because this didn't go how you planned and you want a minute to decide if friendship could work, that's fine. But if you're not sure if you want to try to be friends the same way you weren't sure if you were interested in me, let's just go our separate ways no hard feelings, ya know?*

He said: *I want to be friends.* And then added: *I would be happy for that.*

Okay cool (good choice, I make an adorable friend lol).

I know you will.

Did you want to make a plan to hang out or give it a minute and see what's up down the road?

And just like that he disappeared from the conversation, and I wondered if I'd watched enough Law and Order to be able to get away with murder. Twenty-five minutes later I said: *I guess we'll give it a minute then.*

He came back to say: *Haha. I was doing something else* (which really didn't seem that funny to me) and then: *Not ignoring you*

But I hadn't thought he was ignoring me. I had thought maybe he was uncertain or didn't have the words or couldn't bring himself to answer or hadn't figured out what he wanted, not really, or was just a real piece-of-shit human who didn't care about other people and wasting their time and never gave it a second thought to be in a rapid back and forth conversation only to then disappear for thirty minutes without a heads up. I'd thought a million things, but I hadn't thought he was ignoring me.

I said: *Ok.* And when he said nothing, I added: *Though it seems weird you haven't just answered the question lol.* But I wasn't lol-ing. Jesus, how many times had I used the lol to denote awkward laughter, nervous laughter, I-kind-of-fucking-hate-you-for-making-this-so-uncomfortable-and-difficult-for-me laughter, I-didn't-even-want-to-be-friends-I-don't-know-why-I-offered-you-anything laughter.

Fifteen minutes later he responded with: *Yes let's* and it all kind of fell into place after that. Something like—

(me): *Ok. When are you free? What did you want to do?*
(him): *Free Thursday. We could go to dinner.*
(me): *Sounds great (to both).* (him): *good.*

And then I'd guess we'd just wait and see.

In many ways, the second "date" with Andy was the best one because it one hundred percent confirmed I'd made the right call. I deserved better than Andy without a doubt. I arrived at his place on Thursday night, and we walked to a sushi spot a block away. During the walk, it came up that I earn so little as a writer that my aunt still gives me money in my Christmas card. I'm adult-getting-Christmas-money-poor. It seemed funny in the moment. It seemed less funny when I offered to pay for half (just to be polite) and Andy let me (like a fucking dick).

Back at his apartment, and because I don't drink, Andy offered me a joint he had laying around. Normally, I don't like to smoke with new people and/or men I like but since I no longer liked Andy, I smoked that bad boy without a second thought. Andy plated up all our sushi which was nice (though I would've eaten it out of the containers like an animal but hey that's just me). We watched some adult cartoons (like BoJack Horseman not like hentai) and housed our meals. After I was done, I put my plate down on the coffee table and sat back to enjoy the rest of the show. When the weed had worn off and it felt like a good time to head home, I stood up to use the bathroom before leaving.

"Aren't you going to put your plate in the kitchen?" Andy asked.

"What?" I asked, certain I'd misheard him because he was now standing in the kitchen where presumably he'd just taken his own plate.

"Your plate," he said gesturing.

I was so taken aback that I had to stifle my laughter. There is a certain type of person I cannot stand (okay, there's actually lots but let's just focus on this one type for right now). I cannot stand a bad host. I cannot stand someone who cleans up *during* the party. Cleaning up is for when the guests are gone. Cleaning up during a party is prioritizing cleanliness over the comfort of your guests. It always felt like missing the point to me the same way it does when someone values the food at the party over the people or a parent who reprimands their children in front of their friends. It still reminds me of the time when I was a little kid having dinner over at Dana's house and her mom (who was strict) made a big deal about having elbows on the table. Her dad also threatened to spank me once. Strict parents always really creeped me out because they had all the wrong values. It's a bit like watching a genocide and being worried that someone is swearing like ma'am, you're missing the point.

Anyway, back to Andy and the dinner plates that he wanted me to clean up which felt absolutely fucking insane. This man whom I didn't even want to be friends with, who had pissed away the chance to date (and fuck) me, who had let me pay for my dinner when he should've been trying to get back into my good graces (not to mention him being clearly loaded and me being clearly brokety-broke-broke), this fucking dude wanted me to take my dinner plate into the kitchen instead of just cleaning it up after I left like a normal person (or even just taking it to the kitchen himself when he took his plate or making a second trip like any reasonable person would do).

I took my plate into the kitchen, used his bathroom, and left without much more than a "cya." I nearly skipped back my car certain that I'd just avoided a great calamity. Andy, most certainly, was less than I deserved and while I had had to follow through on our attempt at being friends, it was clear now that even that wasn't worth my time. Andy #3 and I were definitely not meant to be. *Three Andy's and I was out.*

ON ROMANCE

I'll be the first to admit, I've never related to the concept of fairytale romance. At least not in the way they present it in media. When I was a kid, I watched Mr. Dressup and Mr. Rogers which is to say that I learned to like crafting and being kind. Disney movies were not about Romance for me—they were about money and power. I didn't fantasize about being the princess. I never even noticed that they were the ones I was "supposed" to be fantasizing about. In Beauty and the Beast, I didn't want to be Belle. I wanted to be whoever got to live in the castle with the huge library (and talking candlestick). In Cinderella, I wanted singing mice and a fairy godmother. I wanted the magic of a carriage that bursts forth out of a pumpkin. I wanted the satisfaction of the mean girls not winning. That glass shoe looked uncomfortable as fuck and the prince seemed kind of boring.

Looking back over the images of my youth, never once did I identify with the princess. The thing I can't figure out is if that was because of some innate value (unlikely) or something my parents had done to help make me this way (probable).

My parents almost never spoke about my appearance (at least, not during my earliest years). My mom didn't read gossip magazines (though my nana did buy her a yearly Chatelaine magazine subscription) and no one ever spoke about celebrities like they were special. While weight would eventually enter the zeitgeist of our home, it was always couched in terms of health. No one ever romanticized my getting married one day. No one ever spoke about having a husband someday. My dad wanted to me to be a CEO. My mom always knew I'd have higher education. Looking back at my life, I'm not sure I've ever met anyone who didn't think I was capable of doing something. No one has ever doubted me (at least not to my face). Admittedly, that's also a lot to live up to but I say it here so that you understand the path I was set upon.

When I was six or so, I wanted to get a Barbie. Everyone had a Barbie. Barbies were fucking everywhere. My mom wouldn't buy one for me. Instead, I had Rainbow Brite, strawberry shortcake, and My Little Pony. I once begged and begged and begged for a Malibu Barbie, which I think my mom eventually caved on and bought me. But even then, at that early age, I knew there was something my mom really didn't like about Malibu Barbie. I think she thought (the image of) the doll was of an airhead with a bangin' body—something simply not valued in our house.

I had this friend in elementary school whose dad had a home gym. I remember going in there with her and seeing all sorts of really graphic (for a six-year-old) penthouse type posters. All the women were clothed (if only barely). They were greased up and posed in provocative poses. I remember thinking it was so gross. Not just the photos but having to live in a house with that kind of Dad. My childish brain thought it was terrible to have a dad who liked those kinds of photos. But even as a kid, I knew that it was more than that. Liking women who looked sexy wasn't really the problem (not that I fully understood what that meant back then). The rub was having a dad who put them on display. The ick was living with a dad who didn't worry how it would affect his daughter (or his wife if I'm being honest). I imagine he was the kind of dad who would watch the Victoria Secret Fashion Show or the Miss USA pageant, the kind of dad who would gawk at cheerleaders and flirt with the waitress. It should be no surprise that a decade later, it turned out that the kind of dad who puts up lewd posters in his family home, had a second family.

    None of this is to say that my parents were perfect, far from it. But in this one area, in (perhaps accidentally) raising a Feminist daughter, they knew what the fuck was up. It may also have been somewhat accidental and a result of their parents similarly being people of good values. Again, none of my grandparents ever romanticized marriage or talked about me finding a partner someday. And the closest any of them ever got to body shaming me was telling me that if I didn't quit pouting my bottom lip would stay that way (little did nana know how valuable pouty lips would be in the future).

    My parents treated me like a future CEO, someone highly successful and powerful (I sure showed them!). No one ever treated me like a Disney princess. The happiest day of my life was expected to be a graduation of some kind, never a wedding. So, it's hardly any wonder that I didn't grow up fantasizing about being a Disney princess—I didn't want to be rescued, I wanted to live a mansion with books (and probably a talking teapot).

I say all this to try and explain how foreign the idea of romance is to me (because I don't find anything in those movies to be particularly romantic). Nor, going forward, have I ever found the "romance" in modern media to be particularly intriguing. Worth noting, I also think I'm not alone in this at all, but we just don't see it represented in media. There aren't any Hallmark movies where the woman is wooed by wit and support. The movies don't end with a man arranging a graduation shower for his accomplished girlfriend. The movies never seem to showcase the mundanity of a Wednesday night in the life of a couple where he listens excitedly as she talks about her day. For me, romance is a man being invested in your daily happiness.

I've only ever really understood romance in terms of effort and care but that's never really how it's depicted in the media. In media, romance is always based on sex, and if we're being honest, is usually based on how a man can use romance to subdue a woman into having sex with him. A man giving flowers, a man surprising you with jewelry, a man taking you out for a nice dinner or a weekend spa getaway—it's always, whether you want to admit it or not, about "warming her up" and you wouldn't need to be warmed up if it wasn't supposed to lead to sex. Maybe that's my problem with romance (at least in media and how it's contemporarily presented). It's a means to an end and that end rarely leaves the woman satisfied.

That may be a weird take given that this is literally a book in which I fuck (or close to fuck or want to fuck but don't end up fucking) a variety of men. It might seem weird that I'm railing against the thing that's supposed to warm women up and make them want to fuck. But that's because it's less about creating joy for a woman than it is about disarming her defenses against a man. Romance is a rouse (which to be honest, I'd be fine with if we were all on the same page about it). But it's the way we pretend that it's something far less nefarious and far more genuine that I find so fucking outrageous.

Men are given this playbook for romance (buy her flowers, take her out to a fancy dinner, give her a gift) and it's supposed to lead to sex. But it's as if the book was written by men for men (leading to a lot of inaccuracies and misprints). Women are not given their own playbook for romance—they're options are to either buy into this already mis-formed understanding of romance or nothing. Women aren't given a playbook other than the extremely brief advice of withhold sex until you've been given romance. But what happens when you see straight through the façade? How does that change the playbook for women? How are we supposed to know when and when not to fuck? How do we find even one single man who hasn't read the playbook? Who understand that romance is knowing you, respecting you, cherishing you, and has nothing to do with the bullshit you see in the movies. I don't want to be rescued; I want to be thrilled and compensated.

FIRST DATE MAGIC

On the nights that follow a great first date, I go to sleep as early as I can. I take naps in the afternoon. I close my eyes whenever possible. Every detail must be gone over. His soviet-bloc stoicism, how we breathed into each other's mouths, the way his arms negated gravity. Again. Again. No, from the top. Again.

Because there might not be a second date.

This might be as good as it gets and I have to find a way to cherish what is good in this world, while it still feels good. Before I send a text that lands unanswered. Before he decides that I'm not what he wants. Before I become a thing ignored. I gather up all the joy to balance on when I falter. I fill my cheeks for winter and try not to think about the hunger.

The reality is that I know from the beginning with almost every man I date that it's not going to lead anywhere (not that there's anywhere specific I'm trying to go). I know that they're not "the one" (even though I don't believe in the one). They're not going to be a soulmate (even though I don't believe in soulmates). Sometimes they'll surprise me briefly by being better than expected, but it's usually pretty clear from the jump that we'll never have anything more than fun. If even that.

    The problem is that they want one night of fun. I think. I mean, if I'm being honest, I have no fucking idea what they want because the men I date are terrible communicators and/or may not actually even know what they themselves want. They're clearly interested in *some* fun, though *how much* fun often remains unclear, and so I say that they want one night of fun as a place filler because who really fucking knows. I, on the other hand, am looking for 3-8 nights of fun, give or take, the math isn't all that important. I want more fun than they want and that leaves me eternally disappointed no matter how often and readily I put myself back out there. Lately, I've started to wonder whether or not I actually want 3-8 dates of fun or if I've set my sights on that number because it feels like that's the amount of time it takes for a man to realize you're a person and care enough about you (at least on a human level) that he's invested in making you cum. I wonder if cumming is actually all the fun I'm after. None of this really matters though, since they only ever seem to want a little taste of fun, for themselves, as a treat.

    I (mostly) no longer fuck on the first date. Not because I don't want to or care about a man's judgement of my sexual habits. I don't fuck on the first date because I'm giving us both time to want it. I'm giving him time to care about my orgasm, and I'm giving myself time to be interested in him. I don't fuck on the first date to up the chances of a second date. And even then, a second date is rarely a guarantee. This is why after first dates I bathe myself in the endorphins.

Even though I know it's only lust and mostly a projection of who I hope he could be plus a mix of pheromones and the comfort that comes from honestly just having a nice time. Even though I know I would be settling for these men who have so very, very little offer. Even though I know, in many ways, this is all a charade, a circus of the heart to pass the time, little adventures to get my pulse racing on this long hard journey called life. Even though I know this is all just a bit of smoke and mirrors, it's a joy that's rare and so you have to cherish it. I breathe in every last scent of it while it still feels like euphoria.

After a good first date, I am rewiring my own brain. Consciously tracing out pathways of happiness while that's still how they feel. I am terrified to lose this, to become who I am when the disappointment stains my back and I become all too aware just how central men are in my life and how little control I have over whether or not things work out in my favor.

I have to remember, remember, remember. I want to coat my skin in glue. I have to brace and prepare because eventually, predictably, it will all come crashing down around me.

At some point, after a first date, after many first dates that never become second dates, the disappointments will pile onto one another and become unbearable.

The night I go out with Oleg is a good first date. We meet at Starbucks and he's wearing a grey crewneck sweatshirt. When he hugs me hello, he's so much taller that my arms wrap around his waist. He said he was 6'5" and so I should've expected 6'5" but after a lifetime of dating men, you learn not to believe the hype. He pays for our drinks and carries them to a table for us. We talk for an hour, and I notice he rarely drinks his tea. Maybe he takes a sip or two, but it mostly sits there as a gesture until he throws it out when it's time to leave. On the surface it's wasteful, but if that's your first thought consider yourself lucky because it means you've never been on a first date with someone who doesn't order anything. Someone who just sits there staring at you (trying to figure out where they'll bury your body) while you're sipping a coffee and eating a cookie. Men are always doing bonkers shit like this with me. Like they've literally never had a singular thought about social graces or the dynamics of a first date, never considered how their behavior affects others, how they might come off to a stranger. Men are forever not thinking about anything that would make my life easier. But Oleg gets a tea, even though he barely touches it, and because the bar is so goddamn low, it feels like he's a genius and this is a thrilling start to a torrid love affair.

After an hour, I invite him back to the apartment where I'm housesitting. I suggest we watch stand-up comedy (because I always suggest that). We sit on the couch, and I'm laughing but he is not laughing. I wonder if Ukrainian men have less levity in their lives. When I finally ask him about it, he tells me that stand-up moves so quickly it's hard for him to translate fast enough in his head. By the time he understands the joke, the joke is gone. I apologize for not considering this and suggest we watch something of his choosing. He picks The Godfather, which if you're not familiar is one of the longest and quietest movies in existence. During the sixteen-hour screen time, which is so quiet we can hear the city bus going by multiple times, he remains seated beside me without movement. He never puts an arm around me, he never snuggles closer. Even when I get a blanket to put over us because "I'm cold" (reader, I was not cold, he doesn't touch me. I suffer through the longest movie of my life without a single move being placed on me and by the time it's over I'm ready to say goodbye. I stand up before the credits have a chance to roll, expecting to usher him towards the door and berating myself for misreading yet another man, when instead he asks what we're going to watch next.

Next?!?! Was he serious? I'd just sat through the longest, quietest (and honestly truly most boring) movie of my life and he wanted more? Except, forever the naïve optimist, I couldn't help wondering if I was wrong. *Did he just really like the Godfather so much that he didn't want to disrespect it by making out during its artistry? Was he terribly shy and needed just a little longer than a week-long movie to work up the courage to grab a tit?* Because I'm invested (read: I'm an idiot), I start flipping channels.

We spend the next half hour watching SportsCenter, a classic panty-dropper. When still no move is made by the end of the segment, I've worked myself up into quite the little tizzy, practically frothing with something between bafflement and rage. *Why doesn't he want me?! What have we been doing all night?! Doesn't this twenty-five-year-old know I'm hot?!* All the frustration is in vain though because the second the program ends, he turns and kisses me. Clearly, the man just had a genuine respect for media.

We make out on the couch, or more accurately I sit on the couch and he's kneeling in front of me so that our mouths match at the same height. Oleg and so big and strong that for one of the very few times in my life I get to feel small and petite. I know it's fatphobic and sexist, but you can't always help what you love. So, until the media messages of my youth have worn off, I will continue to be turned on by a man's size (in relation to my own). Maybe this is a little version of fairy-tale romance—that bullshit we're taught and unconsciously buy into—that if he's big and tall, then I can be small (like a Disney princess, insidiously).

We move to the bedroom and mess around some more, but we don't fuck because I'm on my period (am I ever not?!?!) and because I don't fuck on first dates anymore. Though, to be honest, I'd fuck Oleg if I wasn't on my period because there's a limited time when I'm housesitting. We mess around until he's ready to come and then I let him jerk off while gazing at my butt cheeks because I'm nice (that's a joke, we all know I'm not nice, but I do have jerk-off-worthy cheeks).

When we're both dressed again, I kiss him goodnight at the front door and go to bed with a smile on my face. The image I have in my mind of Oleg is inaccurate, the way a post-first-date image always is because I don't really know him. I know only the best parts that he chose to show me on the first date. And more than that, I know only the best parts that I've projected and imagined and inserted into my brain about him. Oleg is supremely tall with a broad chest and a master's degree in Political Science from Kyiv University. He had asked me lots of questions and the conversation had flowed easily.

I am already excited for a second date until I find out that he has a roommate and that his roommate is actually a grown man and his teenage son, which means that as soon as I'm done housesitting, and I go back to crashing at my parents as a struggling writer, neither of us will have privacy and nothing can really happen. This is how it ends. Rejection looks different in my dating life, not so much real rejection, or a lack of interest, but the occurrence of obstacles which no one cares enough about to overcome. That's what rejection feels like for me—no one being interested *enough*. Apathetic dating.

I am worried that with every rejection that's not really a rejection (but feels like a rejection), I become a lesser version of myself. Devolving, a spiral of insecurities that present as intellectual thought processes. If I can just figure it out, figure it out, figure it out. If I can just figure *them* out. Every movement is a gesture to change myself into what men want. Not permanently, not forever, just long enough to have some fun. I will become thinner. I will be funnier (so that I'm interesting). I will be less funny (so that I'm not intimidating). I will use creams to keep my skin from sagging. I will be bubbly and smile and appear youthful. I will take charge, make plans, arrange things; I will fucking act my age.

Fuck them better.

Fuck them sooner.

Make them wait.

Stop fucking them altogether.

Maybe I should fuck some of them together?

I get out a pencil and some paper. The numbers might matter in this math. I consider wearing makeup during the day. I will change everything about myself until I can figure out what it is that they fucking want. Then I will change back because it's not who I am. The change is impermanent, a game, social psychology, something to do with your days. I hate both myself and them for every minute of it. My back starts to hurt from all the contorting.

I resent them for caring about the schedule at which I spread my legs, for having to watch the way I carry myself, the way my thighs rub, the sweat underneath my breasts, a more comfortable pair of underwear that I replace halfway through the evening with something sexier just because they might see it. I hate everything I don't understand about them. I hate the notion of playing hard to get because either I like them, and they can have me, or I'm hard to get because I've lost interest. There is no winning. How can I win? How can I figure this out? I can't figure out a fucking thing. I don't know how anyone can possibly expect me to know how to write a loveable narrator when I can't even get a man to ask me on a second date. I am a pariah. This loneliness has alligator skin.

I go out with Hakeem the same week I go out with Oleg. Hakeem was two hours late for our first date, which you'd think meant that there was no date. Looking back, I'm still shocked I didn't immediately take off my makeup when the big hand struck the twelve for the second time. I've never been one to take time-wasting lightly.

Sitting in a restaurant booth, two hours later than I had expected, Hakeem explained what had happened (and at that point I had to take at least a little pity on the guy). The first caveat was that Hakeem didn't actually live here; he was staying with teammates in Surrey during pre-season training and hadn't exactly gotten the hang of the transit system. The man started what he thought would be a short walk to the Skytrain which as it turned out was a bit of a hike (even for a 6'4 professional athlete) taking thirty minutes instead of the five he had been expecting.

Then he had to take one Skytrain and then another Skytrain and finally a Seabus.

The hits kept coming when he arrived in North Van and his phone died. He proceeded to wander around trying to find somewhere to buy a charger (and a place to let him charge his phone) so he could get the address and directions to the apartment not to mention let me know that he'd arrived. All was immediately forgiven (ish, I mean what kind of idiot doesn't map out his route and charge his phone in advance for a big date?)

A twenty-five-year-old, that's who.

We drew a line under it and reset the night. After all, who was I to hold anything other than my body against a young hot professional athlete.

I closed my menu and looked at Hakeem. "What are you going to get to eat?"

"I actually ate before I came, so I'll just get something to drink." And then he took a sip of water from one of those Gatorade bottles athletes are always guzzling from on the field. Like, he'd brought it with him (which seemed both bonkers and, you know, good for him, hydration is important). But now we were sitting at a restaurant, and he was chugging water from a massive (leaking) Gatorade bottle like we were in the second half at the Superbowl.

"Oh," I said dejected. I hate when men act weird on dates. *What am I just going to sit here eating alone? I didn't eat before our date because I knew we were going out for food. Who eats before a dinner date?* I was fucking starving since I was still fully in my "if I don't eat before a date, I'll look thinner" fatphobic-mindset. Newsflash: I'm fat. I'm fat at breakfast and I'm fat at lunch and I'm fat at dinner, even if I didn't eat dinner.

Hakeem looked at me expectantly, "What are *you* going to get?"

"Well, I'm definitely getting something," I said regaining my confidence. I wasn't about to starve because this man was two hours late and had already had dinner. "I'm either going to get this thing or that thing," I said pointing at the menu.

"Get both," he said. And just like that he was back in my good graces. I swear my mouth fell open in impressed surprise. It's not like I was ordering a steak and lobster but still, this must be what it feels like to be a princess or a celebrity or a thin woman without food issues. I told him I couldn't possibly, and he genuinely seemed shocked like he really just wanted me to be full and happy and wasn't that just the sweetest fucking thing you've ever heard. When the waitress came, he ordered a water because his Gatorade bottle was beyond leaking, and I ordered both appetizers and a diet coke.

He told me that he'd gotten a business degree while playing college ball and was now just trying to make it as far as he could in the CFL. I told him about my writing, my hopes for my first book.

"Do you think you'll be famous for your writing or your personality," he asked turning very serious. I loved that my becoming famous was a forgone conclusion to him.

"My writing?" I answered hesitantly.

He shook his head. "Nothing against your writing. I just think you've got this quality." My smile could've lit up the sky. When the bill came, he paid for everything even though he'd only had a water and a few bites of my food and that's the kind of behavior I'm here for. Everything was going perfectly until we realized that the last Seabus would be leaving sooner than we'd expected (because the date had started so late). Cockblocked by public transit.

    I could've offered to drive him home or even let him stay over (but then he'd try to fuck because they always try to fuck, and I didn't want to because I kind of liked him). By which I mean that over the course of our date where I found out his was actually quite intelligent (in addition the accomplished I already knew him to be), I had developed a little crush. Hakeem had gone from potential hookup to guy I might actually want to date in the space of a few hours. Hakeem had gotten in, to his detriment I suppose. We'd had this phenomenal (albeit slightly later than expected) date, and I didn't want to ruin things by fucking too fast. Instead, I drove him back to the Seabus and we made out hot and heavy in the front seat of the car like horny little teenagers fogging up the windows without a care in the world until the very last second. Faces flushed; we waved breathless goodbyes to each other. I was certain we'd see each other again. He texted ten minutes later to say he'd missed the last Seabus.

    Really? I texted.

    Naw just kidding, he replied.

    I went to sleep that night with our date playing on repeat in my head and I wait for the other shoe to drop.

    Hakeem texted the next day which seemed promising, but my hopes were quickly dashed because he had a roommate (which seemed weird because his roommate was just another player on the team—it wasn't like a kid or someone who would be scarred by knowing Hakeem fucks). My mind raced with thoughts of shame—he doesn't want to bring a fat girl over to fuck around with. He doesn't want his roommate to see he likes fat girls. But I remember all too quickly that I'm also old (older than him by a decade), or maybe he's just a private person, or maybe he's supposed to be focusing only on football and practice, or maybe he's sleeping on the couch and doesn't even have a bedroom to himself in which to fuck. It doesn't really matter much in the grand scheme of things. We won't be having a second date. We won't be moving forward. Hakeem, like Oleg before him, will become nothing more than a memory of the magic of a first date, which has a certain beauty to it if you're willing to look for it.

CLOSURE FOR DUMMIES

I once read about a woman who waited eleven days for a man to text, which seemed like a death sentence. I wondered who had taught her to be so open and understanding? From where inside did she pull the strings to make her heart dance so easily to another's beat? To not fold under the weight of it all? To not assume he had little more than a mediocre interest by the second day and, failing that, a lackadaisical distaste by the fifth day seemed a feat of heroism. Who could stand to be so not thought about? To watch the days without wanting pile up along the side of the road.

  Two years later he'll type the words: *I liked you* as if that was a consolation prize. He liked me the same way he liked everyone, lazily, apathetically, whatever. He thought it was important to mention. He thought that I had assumed his lack of lust meant I lacked value, but I'd never thought that. Not really. Maybe sometime. Not mostly. It was hard to fathom so many men (my god, so many!) who couldn't find my company worth their time and desire. They all wanted to fuck me, which only made it worse because it meant that even the fucking couldn't make my (what had to be) terrible personality tolerable.

Andy #1 and I ended things on a Friday night. I was making Bolognese in my parent's kitchen when he texted something low effort like, *how's it going?* It had been two weeks since he'd fed me baby carrots, and I had given him an unreciprocated handjob. He didn't know I'd already lost interest (or it never even occurred to him to care). Men were always dropping the ball and then trying to hand it back to me like, *here, do you want this ball?* and like, *No I don't want that fucking ball. You dropped it on the ground. That ball's dirty.*

Andy wanted to touch base. Andy thought we were still doing something. Andy didn't know he was the first of many Andys. I should've ghosted Andy #1, but I have this sick desire to understand men, or even just people in general, better. I wanted to know what the fuck he could have been thinking. I wanted to know how he could possibly think I was still interested in going out with a man I'd let cum into my chubby little hand and then not text me for two weeks.

The real dummy in this scenario is me, though. It's always me. Because how could I ever expect the kind of man who behaves this way to have both the self-awareness and eloquence to be able to explain himself. Instead, he said something about a busy schedule and how he liked me and blah blah blah who cares. I thanked him (a true Canadian at heart) for taking the time to answer and went back to my bubbling Bolognese. We never spoke again. The Bolognese was delicious. The secret is adding milk.

When Andy #2 and I stopped seeing each other, it could've been a mutual ghost. I should've let it be a mutual ghost, but I prefer a severed head. Whenever anything ends with a man, I have this delusional hope that I'll be able to gain some kind of knowledge in the closure. By the time things are ending, my desires are not about keeping a man but instead enjoying the fruits of an exit interview. I mean, can you imagine a man giving you the exact reasons why he didn't like you or didn't want to see you again? List three things, my guy—I would legit cum. Which isn't to say that I would change a damn thing about myself based on the opinion of a man, but wouldn't it be kind of fun to know, to have the undeniable facts (of someone else's perspective) or to be able to pinpoint the exact moment things had gone wrong?

Sadly, closure comes about as often as a woman having casual sex (spoiler alert: almost never). But that's never stopped me from trying. And so, because I wanted closure with Andy #2, and you can't just outright ask someone why they haven't been texting you, I had to start the conversation off with a rouse. I asked Andy #2 if he wanted to hang out again and poised my fingers with follow-up questions for when he said no. Andy #2 said that he wasn't looking for anything serious and couldn't hang out because he was pretty busy until August (it was currently May) what with being in Mexico and all. Talk about an overreaction—you didn't have to leave the country bro; I can take a hint. Andy #2 and I never spoke again, except to add each other on facebook. LOLZ.

Jokes about country-fleeing aside, Andy #2 was no aberration in that he had obviously and vastly overestimated my interest. I just wanted to hear his side of the few dates we'd been on; I wasn't trying to be his girlfriend. Men were constantly overestimating my attraction, my desire, my feelings for them, and the level of commitment that interested me. To men, it seemed, there were only ever two options for how to treat a woman—like a whore who should just take your lame dick that won't even get her off, or a future wife. There was no in-between.

And don't even get me started on just being honest with us, especially in rejections. My whole life, men have been described as being logical, methodical, the ones with the objective brains and ability to control their feelings, but I've never met a man like that. Men are honestly the most hysterical of all the bitches. Unable to take a joke, unable to see themselves and what they have to offer clearly, unable to take criticism and improve their behavior, unable to communicate and simply be honest. To me, it seemed that men were as scared of a harmless negative interaction with a woman as women were afraid of a violent physical altercation with a man. This was especially true when it came to men online—men I'd never even met yet.

"I don't want a relationship!" I can hear them yelling through the internet. "I just got out of a— "

"I'm not looking for anything serious becau—"

I cut them off, "I don't need the backstory." There is no explanation that makes this abrupt excitation seem anything other than insane. Why do men feel the need to make this declaration as if I had asked? As if I had asked a stranger on the internet for a deep and committed relationship before even seeing a social media profile, or at bare minimum a picture in which they're smiling (not just holding up a fish, face mostly hidden under a ball cap). As if I had tied my hands around their neck and their hands around their back and demanded them to march.

A man blurts because he's afraid—he has a terrible, terrible fear that a woman might get the wrong idea and fail to notice his attentions are ill-intentioned. As if that was one of the great crimes in the world. I worry about rape and poverty and injustice, and he is consumed by the terror of being loved, of something ending badly. He says, "I don't want to lead you on, I don't want you to get hurt." But let's be honest that he is not so concerned with saving me hurt as he is with saving himself the hassle. He demeans my intelligence with his assumptions—to think I would fall for a fool such as him.

"Ain't nobody trying to love you, kid." I say.

His parents did a terrible job. The only phone number I want is theirs, the customer complaint department, please.

I had a conversation once with one of the extremely few male friends I've had in my life. It was years after first-year university (back when I had had an entire double room to myself). Jeff told me that he had thought I'd liked him, had wanted to fuck him, because I told him if he ever came out to UBC for a visit that he could stay in my room. He thought I was hitting on him. I had two beds and thought we were friends, was just trying to be friends. I hadn't even had sex at that point, I'd barely even kissed that many boys. I could live without Jeff in my life but the pattern, this totally bonkers way that men always assume I'm far more interested than I am, has infuriated me my entire life. It's an irritant because it often meant that men ended things prematurely—they liked me, just not enough to have a relationship with. The bizarre part being that I'm almost never trying to have a relationship with them. I just wanted to go on some dates, hang out and have some makeouts, maybe fuck, maybe not, and then maybe even just end up as friends (like actual friends) or whatever. But all these men I was dating were getting one or two dates in and thinking I wanted so much more than them (though I'd never, honestly never, indicated I did) so they'd end things early (or act so nonchalantly as to not give me the wrong impression that I'd lose the tiniest interest I had). Often, months or years later they'd try to circle back around. Sometimes the come-back-charlie-ness of it all was fine (because they were hot enough for me not to care, but honestly how often are they that hot?).

And then there was the deeper issue, which bothered me far more and enraged me beyond imagination, the fucking audacity they had to think I'd care that much about them (outside of the way I care about humans in general). These men, ending things after two dates because they didn't want to lead me on and it's like *lead me on to what?* A relationship with some mediocre and not at all standout-ish man? Hard pass bro. The overconfidence made me want to vomit in my mouth a little. The way men are raised to think they're just so goddamn special and have something to offer because what? They have a job and haven't murdered anyone? My guy, you can't even tell a dad joke let alone make me laugh until I pee, and you think I'm limiting my options for you? Dating men is exhausting. The way they forgive themselves so easily is truly intolerable.

Things with Oleg and Hakeem didn't end because they thought I wanted a relationship (though both absolutely asked me if that's what I was looking for prior to meeting because we live in a world where that's the default for women—a relationship that leads to marriage). I couldn't be less interested in ever getting married. The irony of which was not lost on me as man after man presumed that was my goal.

Things with Oleg and Hakeem ended because of a lack of privacy. None of us had the freedom to fuck. Once the sting of disappointment (over not getting what I wanted) dissipated, they both remained in my memory as first date magic. But first dates are rarely the truth about anyone. First dates are who you are when you put your best foot forward (if you have any fucking sense). First dates are terribly deceptive, because they let you feel like you've met the other person, that you know something about them, but you don't really. You don't know anything real. You don't know anything beyond the fact that they could make decent conversation (maybe) and we're attractive (enough) that you'd probably be willing to make out with them and/or have a second date (maybe even get a little naked, it all depends). But your time together on that first date isn't an indication of who they are or even how well you'd get along because everyone is acting in the beginning. Everyone is biting their tongue. Everyone is keeping all their bullshit and darkness and idiotic ideas to themselves on a first date. I know this as fact because men are forever circling back to me long after our first and second dates to reveal themselves.

Two years after our first dates, in the same exact month as before, Oleg and Hakeem both circle back around. I'd gone out with both of them in the space of a week and then saw neither again. Yet, here they were again, both texting me to reconnect, in February. It truly is the coldest month to have both these boys reaching out in the same moment for chubbier comforts. They both say hello. They both want to hang out again. I am no longer interested in dating, but I'm housesitting, and I want to fuck. I'm horny and I want to fuck, and I want to kiss, and I want to feel hot, and I want validation. And so,

I fuck them both within two weeks of each other. The sex is disappointing with both. They both cum, and I do not cum with either. I might've been able to if this was my apartment and I wasn't housesitting and I had access to a vibrator to get me off while being fucked. But this is not my apartment and I do not have my vibrator and they're both bad in bed (in so much as everyone who doesn't prioritize the female orgasm is bad in bed) and so we fuck, but I don't cum because neither go down on me, and I don't ask either to go down on me. Seeing them again is also a disappointment simply because the magic of our first date has worn off. They are not the men that I remembered. They are not the men I had fantasized them to be. They were more timid, less self-assured, less confident, less charismatic, far less interesting. But I am a woman and disappointing sexual encounters is our legacy, so I brush it off and don't bother texting them again. This time it is more than a lack of privacy that ends things.

STUFFED CHICKEN AND TOSSED SALAD

Michael was a Nice Guy™ in so much as he absolutely thought he was a sweetheart but was actually kind of a dick. When he opened the door of his apartment, I could tell right away that he was shorter than his profile had said. He'd written that he was 5'10 but he was 5'8 if he was an inch. Women (especially fat women) spend our whole lives making sure men online don't think we're hiding anything from them, and men have the audacity to mislead us about their height as if we won't notice, as if being eye to eye with a man who'd said he was 5'10 when you're 5'7 isn't jarring.

    I stayed because I had already done my hair and makeup and driven over to his place for a homecooked meal. I know I should've left. *Don't you think I know that I should've left?* But I had put in effort, and I had driven all this way. One thing I'll tell you though is that it's not that easy to laugh in someone's face. It's not intuitive to turn around the second someone has opened the door to you. It's not unique to be a woman and a people pleaser and to hope for the best even once the disappointments have started. One day I will leave a date when a man has lied about something. One day, I will take myself out alone instead of settling for dishonesty disguised as an accident. One day I will wash the makeup off my face and put up the hair I'd spent half an hour on instead saving the feelings of a man. Because, and this is some brutal honesty here, I'm not sure a first date that started with a lie has ever gotten any better. It's so boring how predictable they are.

Michael wore a button-down shirt and skin-tight jeans with cowboy boots, which to be honest was kind of hot and did lessen the sting of his having lied about his height. He ushered me inside to have a seat on the couch while he poured me a diet coke. He made an alcoholic drink for himself which in theory was fine, encouraged even. In many ways, I prefer a man having a drink or two on a date because it lets them loosen up and become more fun. But things can really go left once you open those floodgates—I've yet to meet a person who doesn't think they're more interesting and fun when they're drunk, but I'm here to tell you that most of you are worse—especially men. It sounds sexist to make such a generalization but based on the anecdotal evidence of my dating life, men do not get better with alcohol (nor marijuana while we're on the subject). They usually get louder and sloppier and more open in the worst ways possible. With each drink, they gain an unearned confidence in their wit and behavior (as if straight white men weren't already too full of their own hype). Men tend to relax after that first drink and that's when they get you hooked. It rarely stops after one, though, and somewhere between the second and third cocktail, things usually take a turn for the worst. They stop reading social cues and body signals (if they were ever really reading them before). They become their true selves and if we're being honest here, most men should keep that guy tucked away (far, far away).

Michael and I played cards while dinner finished cooking and I genuinely had fun. He was surprised by how good I was at crib, and I was just happy to be doing something fun on a date. I think about this often, how many times a woman is having fun on a date simply because she's having fun on a date (not because the man is special, or the connection is great but just because she's a person doing a fun thing and leaning into it). That's the thing about dating as a cishet woman, it's a lot about being a good sport. I know the way I talk about men makes me sound bitter, but I'll be completely honest in that I think that's because society has conditioned us to see women complaining as inherently untrustworthy and inaccurately dramatic. I mean, it's not like he was murdering me, right? So, what's my fucking issue, yeah? My issue is how disappointing and lame men (read: men I've dated) have turned out to be. I say turned out because isn't that what every movie and tv show and book has been trying to tell us—how great men are? The only great man I know is my dad, and if we're being honest, I still had to train him to ask reciprocal questions in conversation.

When the timer for the chicken went off, Michael jumped up spilling his third drink just a little. He'd made stuffed chicken and rice with vegetables. He gave me my plate first and then went to the washroom. A few minutes later Michael emerged wearing sweatpants. He'd changed into sweatpants to be more comfortable. I couldn't help but wonder if this is why he'd invited me over, why he'd offered to make us dinner rather than going to a restaurant, so that he could have an outfit change.

Some people like sweatpants on men. Not me though, and not this early (for the love of God!). We hadn't even kissed yet and he was already this comfortable? I couldn't help feeling slighted somehow, like I wasn't worth wearing his best outfit for the duration of an evening. Not that his opinion of my worth had any effect on how I viewed my own worth. I was worth the tightest jeans in the world. I was worth his nuts sweating and his dick being crushed a bit. I was worth his discomfort. Of that, I was certain.

When I called him out for his mid-date outfit change, he laughed and seemed genuinely embarrassed. I should've known not to trust his interpretation of the situation though. Men are never ashamed of anything except their dick size. No matter how much I want them to be ashamed of all the stupid things they say, their cruelty, their inconsideration, their misogyny—they never are. But tell a man his dick is trash and just this once you'll hit a nerve. Not that I said anything about his dick, I was too busy leaning into the date—trying to have first date magic. I had ignored the lie about his height, and now I was ignoring his outfit change. The chicken he'd made was good and the cards had been fun, and I was horny and bored and ever hopeful of meeting a man to have an ongoing situationship with so that I might be able to have an orgasm every so often, you know, as a treat.

But that's the thing with first dates and leaning in. Sometimes you lean too hard and too fast and suddenly you're making out with this dude who changed into sweatpants mid-way through your first date, and you're on the couch in his living room which is actually only a foot or two away from his bed in this fancy but still just-a-studio apartment. And before you know it, the two of you move to his bed. You move to the bed of this man who hasn't impressed you, and whom you're basically tolerating because you're a bit of a slut (in a good way), and he did make you a nice stuffed chicken dinner, and you did have some laughs playing cards prior to his second drink and now he's a bit sloppy so the making out, which had started out hot, but is now tepid and on the few steps it takes to move from the couch to the bed, he's taken off his shirt and his sweatpants (under which he is full commando) and is now completely naked in front of you. *Or does this kind of shit just happen to me?*

So, Michael hasn't taken off any of my clothes (which I guess is fine because honestly, I was good with just making out) and now everything is so weird and awkward and maybe it's because he'd had those two-and-a-bit drinks, but he doesn't even notice. I give him the grace of alcohol as an excuse but it's also entirely possible that he doesn't notice because this is his personality and he's an inconsiderate piece of shit.

There isn't time to think because Michael catches me off guard by wrapping his arms around me and falling back onto the bed, pulling me on top of him. I can't help but think about whether he's going to get precum all over my dress. We're still kissing but it's awkward (for me, I'm not sure he even notices) and I'm not in a comfortable position, so I try to roll off him nonchalantly and take a breath. Lying beside Michael I look at him and this situation I'm in and think about how I'm just so fucking bored of men these days and wouldn't it just be amazing if I could find another, better guy to fuck around with when I'm in the mood, but because I've already met this guy, even though he's kind of a loser, he's gotten in ahead of all the other hypothetical guys I'll have to sort through if I decide to toss him in the trash. So, I hike my dress up a bit, push him back on the bed, kiss down his chest and start sucking his dick like a pro. I know, of course, that I could take off my own clothes but before I can even ask myself if I'd like to do that, he's hooked his arms behind his knees and, for lack of a better expression, is aiming his asshole right at me hoping I'll toss his salad without ever having to even ask.

It's not even the act of eating ass itself that bothers me (I'm not here to kink-shame). It's the fucking audacity, the absolute unmitigated gall, of a man who's basically been a disappointment all night to be aggressively pointing his asshole in my face that cannot be tolerated. There's that saying about a straw breaking the camel's back, and as it turns out, it was a literal asshole that broke mine. And just like that, I stood up from where I'd been crouching at the end of his bed, looked smugly down at him lying there on his bed with his knees up near his ears and told him I had to go. I grabbed my purse and was out the door before he'd had a chance to pull his sweatpants back on.

Driving home I'm furious and wonder if I should stop dating men. I'm worried I've fucked too many ordinary boys. I'm worried that I kissed away my heart and my belief in the worth of people. I'm worried that I'm filled with a bitterness that can't be washed off. I can't think my way out of this place. I reach for my purse at a stoplight. I check all the pockets for something I can't find. I fear I've left my last shred of dignity at the foot of Michael's bed. The light turns green, and I remember who the fuck I am. This shame belongs to Michael, not me.

POKER FACE

We type mostly in emojis. We tell stories to each other in characters designed to save us time, and by the time I'm agreeing to meet we know almost nothing about each other. Except that he has made me laugh and for now that is enough.

It is enough until I remember (how the fuck could I ever forget?) that I am a thirty-three-year-old wanna-be writer who lives with her parents, and he is a twenty-three-year-old I-don't-know-what who may or may not live with his parents and suddenly his living situation becomes the most important thing.

I'm not looking to hook up but if the first date (meet, meet-cute, *why don't we just meet?*, "We could just meet up real quick," he says) goes well and there's another date/night/hang, we would need a place to just *be,* eventually. I am too old to be making out on street corners and in cars.

Eventually is more important now. I don't have time (I have tons of time) to take leaps. I can't be bothered putting in effort to meet men that I cannot date (even though I'm on Tinder, which apparently isn't for dating or is for dating depending on who you ask, and I no longer know who to ask). I am a thirty-three-year-old wanna-be writer who lives with her parents. I don't have time to date men without apartments. I don't have time to date men when I should be writing. Oh god, why am I even trying to date? I have more degrees than men who have ever loved me, and I'm a thirty-three-year-old wanna-be writer who lives with her parents.

What kind of writing do you do? They ask using far fewer characters and in sentences that have to be pieced together like leftover muffin crumbs between the pads of my fingers. I tell them *I write about sex and dating* because it's too hard to explain that *I write about what it's like to be a fat woman in this world*, and *I write about myself* sounds terribly naïve and indulgent (which it is). A professor I had back at Concordia once called it chicklit. He said I could do better than chicklit. What he meant was the piece wasn't good enough, wasn't witty enough but he used the backs of women to stand up and say this; it probably read far too much like a diary (which is just called a journal if you're a man). When men write about sex, it's important (you better sit up and listen!). But I'm just a woman writing about sex (with men, unfortunately). A friend asks why I can't seem to decentralize men from my life. Except that they're not really that central, but I can't tell people the truth, which is that of course I want to go on all these great adventures, but dating is free, and travel is expensive, and life gets lonely and every so often a girl would like to have an orgasm that she didn't entirely orchestrate herself.

So even though it's Monday, and Monday is when I had said we would meet, I go to the gym. I send a message and ask what he does for a living.

He says: *I am an equity analyst. Or one could also say that I simply play cards. Depends on the mood.*

I ask: *Which one is metaphorical and which one literal?* though I already know. He is a poker player, which feels sketchy (which in turn feels judgmental). I ask him if he lives alone and when he says no, I don't mince words.

I say: *Ooph, well that ends that I guess, I don't live alone either* because whatthefuckisthepoint anymore.

He says: *Simply the beginning my dear* and we banter back and forth while he tries to convince me that there is a solution to every problem, and I eventually forget that I am a grown woman who has made out in far too many cars and on far too many street corners and that some problems are just big fucking problems, and some solutions aren't worth the effort.

He says: *Best Western has never saved the day before but maybe today is a special day.*

I say: *I'm not looking for a hookup so a one-off in a hotel isn't really for me.* I don't add that I'm a wanna-be writer living with her parents and that if I had money for a hotel I wouldn't be squatting here. I don't add that I would never be willing to pay half on a hotel room (again) for sex. I don't add that my feminism is flawed and my ideas of equality ill-defined and that I am thirty-three and he is twenty-three and this all seems too complicated and filled with shame.

I say: *Sorry I don't mean to rain on your parade. I just don't want to waste your time.* I'm trying to tell him no. I'm trying to end this before it starts.

He says: *No parade raining has happened quite yet. I'm not sure what the answers to the universe's more life-threatening issues are, but I feel as though this conundrum we are faced with is something that could be overcome. Time wasting is certainly not what I intend to do though, so I hope you will be gentle but firm in the way you tell me to hit the road, jack.*

I read this between sets at the gym and he gets in a little. His use of commas and full sentences are a baited hook. Somewhere in between reps, he sneaks in with wordplay. And just like that, we're meeting. I rush home from the gym. I rush to get ready. I text and say that we need to go for food—I try not to yell it through the screen.

He says something about having eaten recently, which I take as soft rejection. He says something about not wanting to go somewhere too expensive, which I take as an undervaluing of my time and my very being. Every text is a reason I should bail. I say as much. Again, he convinces me that nothing is a real problem. Again, he sways me. My hair and makeup are already done. I ask where we should meet.

We meet near his house. I pick him up like a mom after school (or a normal nice person doing something nice and normal for someone else). But nothing feels so nice and normal.

He says *turn right at King Edward and Hudson, I'll be there*. But when I get there, he is not there. *Oops*, he says, *drive one more block up King Ed and I'll be there in one minute.* So, I do. And he is not there. And then he is there.

He gets into my car, and we drive down Granville and park. Inside the entrance of the restaurant, I ask him to get us a table while I use the washroom. When I come out, he tells me that they're closed—no food. We walk up the street to another restaurant where they tell us that their kitchen is also closed. The city is asleep before I've even had dinner. They say, "You can have drinks," and so we go inside where I order a diet coke and he orders a water, and I'm no longer sure why anyone in this world continues to exist.

He tells a story about his brother's wedding in some Massachusetts town I've never heard of. He says it was in this one place and then, no, it was in this other place. Or was it in the first place?

"It's very important that we figure out the details," I say, and he laughs and the rumble in my belly is no longer as loud. We start to joke back and forth. We start to have fun. He tells me about his job, how he travels all over the place: Barcelona, Monte Carlo, Australia.

"That's why it makes sense to live at home," he says, though it doesn't completely. It makes sense to be twenty-three and living at home if you need to. He's not in school, he says, just the poker. He doesn't say too much outside of what I ask about his job. But I'm hardly in a place to judge someone living with their parents. He says again, "That's why it makes sense to live at home because I'm travelling and away so often." He says he spent a few months in Australia last year. He says he goes to Monte Carlo all the time. It's all very impressive.

When the conversation turns to dating, he tells me that he dressed up for our date by wearing jeans and a t-shirt.

"What would you normally be wearing?"

"Shorts."

"Like short shorts or like swim trunks?"

"Swim trunks, with the built-in underwear."

"Who doesn't love a bit of mesh," I smile. This is the extent of my flirting.

He agrees about the mesh and again laughter pushes us towards each other. He pays the bill. I offer to drive him home.

When we pull over in front of where I had picked him up, he asks if I want to smoke the joint he brought. He lingers in the passenger seat and doesn't open his door right away.

Sure, I say, "We could walk around." I don't want to get high though. I don't know how long we will be walking for. I don't want to get trapped here, walking around in the summer heat, with nowhere to go, just a couple of over-aged teenagers still living with their parents for very different or totally similar reasons (I'm still not sure which).

We walk and talk about Tinder. I'm only the second person he's ever met, which seems like bullshit. I've met so many men, or have I? I've talked to hundreds, wasted my time on thousands, listened to a billion wax-poetic about tits and tell me all about how they're fresh out of relationships. Tinder is all your ex-boyfriends, broken like records. "And how was it?" I ask about the other girl, the one he said he'd met in Australia.

"It was great," he said, and I tried not to be jealous of a woman on another continent. He asked what I was looking for.

"Dating."

"Dating and then hopefully...?" he made a sweeping gesture at nothing with his hands.

"No hopefully," I cut him off. "Just dating."

He looked at me like that was impossible. Was it hard to believe because I was a woman or because I was a woman during/past marriageable/childbearing years? Did he think I was hanging out with twenty-three-year-olds for that super dope baby batter?

"Just dating," I reiterated. "You?"

"Fucking."

Well, shit. "Fucking and activities or just fucking?" It had started to seem so weird asking this question. I mean, did I have so few friends to do fun things with that I had to stoop to spending my time trying to convince these men with their dicks (practically in their hands, panting, ready to fuck me), to just maybe shoot some pool or eat a meal or treat me in any way that suggested even the tiniest possibility that I might be more than just a walking vagina? Why didn't any of them want the non-sex fun too? Were all their friends just super fun and always available? I was starting to think that the reason people got married had little to do with love and instead was entirely about always having someone to hang out with. This logic was not lost on me. My life was filled with family and friends whom I loved, and not a single fucking person to hang out with.

"I don't care how much time is spent in and around the fucking," he said, and he seemed to mean it but then again, they always seem to mean it. I took him at his word, but what kind of idiot takes a twenty-three-year-old at his word?

"Do you usually date older women?" I asked like a broken record, like a needy baby, like a girl standing in front of a parking lot attendant just trying to get some goddamn validation. I don't know what I wanted him to say. *Yes*? That he had dated a hundred women slowly creeping towards the open arms of death in order to make me just another old lady in a line of cougars? Did I want him to answer *no* in order to make me an outlier, to make me unique, which would then come with its own set of problems like—would he like my sagging boobs? Would he expect me to teach him new things? Was I supposed to be the dominant one or was he supposed to lead the way? Was age or gender the trump card? Was I going to be just another first in life, just another thing he sampled and then passed over? I wanted him to say that I seemed great. Walking around his parents' neighborhood (presumably the one he'd grown up in), I wanted him to say that I seemed goddamn amazing and though he wasn't sure what would happen with us, he didn't want to miss his chance. I wanted him to see that I was great, right off the bat.

He said, "You seem really insecure about the age difference," and just left it hanging there. But I wasn't insecure about the age difference. I was insecure about all the things I thought a thirty-three-year-old was supposed to have: a job, an apartment, a reasonable expectation of paying off their student loan. I had none of these things. I was a writer. I was a writer. I kept trying to tell everyone that I was a writer.

I just finished my master's degree—I would type followed immediately by—*and I'm (trying to be) a writer.* Some days it seemed cute and self-deprecating; other days it just seemed pathetic and unrealistic. And that didn't even address the other stretch of truth in the sentence. A stretch so deep I practically had to start doing yoga just so I could tell it. *Just? Just finished my master's degree?* I had finished my degree in April and here it was another April and September later and I was still saying *just*. Like, who me? living at home with my parents, yeah, I *just* moved back, I *just* finished my degree, I'm *just* a little bit of a disappointment to my parents, I'm *just* hanging on by a thread, I'm *just* trying to survive. And maybe it wouldn't matter to them, wouldn't matter to any of them, but Jesus, did it matter to me. It was the only reason I hadn't changed my phone number since moving back to

Vancouver, so that every new guy I gave my number to would ask, "514? What area code is that?" and then I'd say Montreal and add that that was where I had earned my master's degree and hadn't bothered to change it back. *Just* a little stretch of the truth.

Twenty minutes later, he'd convinced me to go back to his parents' house having explained that they were actually out of town for the weekend. His parents' house looked like a show home—fancy art, coffee table books, not a scrap of mail or paper or regular countertop mess anywhere. I guess being rich means having enough drawers to hide your crap (and cleaning ladies to put it all away for you). They definitely had cleaning ladies. His mother was a doctor after all. Which shouldn't have but made me like him more.

In the den in his parents' house, we sat on an L shaped couch, and I tried to fold my legs up under me without looking weird. I sat facing where I thought we would be watching tv until he said he didn't know where the remote was (and I couldn't figure out if they were so rich, he never came into this room, or we had just nonchalantly broken into someone else's home). We sat in the dark and I wished I had smoked the joint with him. But I hadn't been convinced then. It felt so embarrassing to go back to his parents' house (embarrassing for me, I mean, he was just a kid, so for him it felt normal).

In the den, he introduces me to Lil Dicky's music and we make out. His kissing is okay but not great, either because he's young or inexperienced or both. He doesn't open his mouth the right amount. His lips feel too hard or tight or wrapped around his teeth. I spend the next half hour trying to get him to gently suck and pull at my bottom lip. I do this for me, to make it more enjoyable for me—I'm not trying to teach him anything. I'm not trying to be the older woman. I'm just trying to be a person he might like. I'm just trying to experience some pleasure. He doesn't know I'm not going to fuck him tonight.

The kissing finally becomes much more enjoyable and then we're just two kids who still live with their parents making out in the den like teenagers. I think about maybe blowing him but then my eye starts to water, and I decide not tonight. I should choose not to suck his dick because I have my period so there's zero chance he'd be reciprocating. I should choose not to suck his dick because why should he get an orgasm when I won't. I should choose not to suck his dick for a hundred different reasons. But I choose not to do it because sometimes my eye waters for no reason and I'm worried it'll fuck up my makeup and it'll be embarrassing to explain that I have some defect or infection or something gross like a single goddamn tear streaming down my face and you just cannot trust that a man will treat you kindly.

But why would you be fucking around with a dude who wouldn't? Honestly reader, I don't need that kind of judgement from you right now.

And so around 3am, when it feels like I can't keep blinking away this saline nightmare, I say that I have to go. "It's late," I say, and he says, "really?" and then walks me to the door. I don't tell him I have my period. I don't talk about my watery eye. I don't say I don't want to fuck you on the first date because I've learned that most men need a few dates to give enough of a shit about me to not treat me terribly after putting their dicks inside me.

Standing at his front door, him on the inside, me a small step down outside, I turn around to face him. I do this thing when I say goodbye, and I don't know why I do it. Well, that's not true. I do it because I want to and because it seems cute and it feels sexy and greedy and I always think it'll be adorable, but they never seem to think it's adorable. It never goes over how I want. So, when he walks me to the door and I step outside and then turn back around to gently tug at his shirt and pull him in for another kiss, I shouldn't. I do, but I shouldn't. Because he doesn't look at me like he's found some amazing woman who's rocked his world and is brilliant and hot and whatever the fuck it is that men, or boys, are looking for. He looks at me like he's confused and hurt and hadn't wanted the night to end and doesn't understand why I have to leave because I guess maybe he expected that we would fuck, and I don't want to fuck him yet and probably not in his parents' house and definitely not on the first date, though Best Western no longer seems so entirely out of the question. But pulling him in for a last kiss feels like sending the last text message. The ball rolls away from my court. The high ground disappears beneath me. I mentally kick myself.

Back home, I google his name and the word "Poker," which seems entirely too vague to bring up any results. But things are not as expected and there is a great return on my investment—pictures of him sitting behind a pile of money (millions of dollars I'll learn upon further reading). I have to remind myself that men are not their jobs. I have to remind myself to be careful not to fall in love with their careers, the adventures they have and instead that I must have my own. I think, if I cannot be everything (gambler, pro baller, Ukrainian politico) …then perhaps I can capture a glimpse by dating them. With only one life to live, surely there isn't enough time to live out a thousand story lines, but I can trace them, on the palms of men, with their hands on my hips and my lips tickled by their breath. Men are never as great as their careers paint them to be. This is a lesson I learn (and then forget) over and over and over again.

Every few days after our good first date, when he hasn't contacted me, I google his name, select *news*, and wait to see. I watch a few old videos of him where he remains calm and aloof. Still, he doesn't text me to hang out again. He doesn't express an interest in me. I think ahh yes, this is a poker face, this is why he is so good.

Soft rejection (read: ghosting) is where the story should end but that's rarely where it ends. Men live to circle back. A few years later, he texts out of the blue. He messages to say that he's sorry for treating me so poorly. He messages to say that he's sorry and that I deserved better and could he take me out to dinner. He messages to say *please* and shows real remorse, I think. You can never be sure with men. Or maybe you can, but not after only one date and several years of silence. But I'm an optimist, however naïve, so I believe him.

At dinner he apologizes, and we eat from multiple plates (my favorite activity). We make out later that night and a few other nights after. We fuck once or twice. It's okay. It's whatever. By which I mean I don't cum.

After I move to Montreal and have had my sexual revolution (more on this later), I return at Christmas and go over to his place to hookup. Within ten minutes of making out, when I can tell he thinks we're going to fuck, I ask if he likes eating pussy. I ask as a way to suggest that he should lick my pussy and make me cum. I am taken aback when he says not really and looks at me nervously. I know he thinks we're still going to fuck but I am a different woman now. This time I get dressed and leave. We don't fuck. We don't have disappointing sex. I don't fuck men who don't lick pussy. No exceptions (now).

GOOD VIBRATIONS

JP and I met through Blackplanet when I was twenty-one and he was nineteen. God, we were young and stupid. We used to fuck in the backseat of my car, down deserted lanes, and poorly lit backroads. Both living with our parents, we lacked life experience and the space to fuck in privacy. Though I'm not sure how much privacy would've even made of a difference to the quality of the sex back then. We fucked maybe twenty times, and I never once came. He'd bust after a few thrusts. We barely even took off our clothes.

When I was twenty-one, I was still drinking and fucking men for validation. Their desire meant that I was desirable and even though I wasn't getting orgasms, sex with men was making up for all the times I hadn't felt attractive. JP was hot and fucking him meant that I too had to be hot. My logic about this was flawless (what can I say I was blitzed!). The truth is that I was fucking JP because he made me feel hot and wanted and because I was still drinking (and making terrible decisions) and because I was bored (story of my life!). I was fucking JP because the kissing was enjoyable, and he always came quickly so the making out was most of the sexual encounter anyways. I'm pretty sure I'd yet to actually cum from anything other than masturbation at this point in my life but if I had, it certainly wasn't a regular occurrence. So, while I've always known it was unfair that I wasn't cumming during sexual encounters, I didn't yet know the whole extent of it. I didn't yet know why I wasn't demanding it (but I am certain that the quietness of my voice was absolutely based in internalized fatphobia).

When I was twenty-one sharing stories with girlfriends the next morning, we didn't ask if you came from a hookup. We didn't even think to ask, it was such a forgone conclusion that you didn't. I do remember that I used to tell men that I wouldn't suck their dicks during a casual encounter, claiming something like, "that's just for boyfriends." I doubt I had it so solidly figured out back then, but I knew that men were never going down during casual sex so why the fuck should I? They were lucky I even let them fuck and that was purely the fault of beauty culture and fatphobia and our fucked up patriarchal society that devalues the female orgasm and makes sure little girls don't have enough confidence and certainty in themselves to ask for what they want (until their thirties, if not later). And like I said, because I was drinking. We stopped fucking when I met the (once thought to be) love of my life. It'd be a few more years before I'd stop drinking (what can I say, all bad habits rarely end at once).

Ten years later, when I was studying for the GRE and finishing up my second BA in preparation for going to grad school, JP and I matched on Tinder. I invited him over to my dorm room (think apartment building with all college kids not those single rooms with twin size beds and communal bathrooms). We got down to business pretty quickly because I was busy with school and exam prep (and it's not like he had much to say). It felt like a lifetime had gone by since we'd last hooked up, two nearly-still-teenagers in the backseat of a car. That night in my on-campus apartment, he showed up to fuck without bringing any condoms. It would seem that while I had developed in the last decade, he was still young, dumb, and full of cum.

I didn't normally keep condoms on hand. I was already doing all the heavy lifting when it came to men, brining condoms were the absolute bare minimum they could do. If any other man had shown up without condoms, I would've kicked him to the curb for his ill-thought-out plan. Luckily, I had some novelty condoms I'd had made previously for my birthday. I don't remember what they said, but I remember thinking they were hilarious at the time. JP was able to get the condom on, but it was clearly too tight (which only bothered me to the extent that I worried it would break). It was weird to fuck JP on a bed. It was weird to fuck someone who I'd fucked dozens of times before but who'd never seen me completely naked. Perhaps the weirdest of all the new things I was experiencing that night was that I had planned to prioritize my own orgasm. Before JP arrived, I'd put my vibrator on my nightstand. I moved it from being hidden under my pillow so that there would be no surprises, no confusion—I was putting it all out there without even a whiff of shame.

With nearly a decade and a half of mostly unsatisfactory sex under my belt, this night with JP was destined to have a much greater purpose. I was going to fuck JP and get mine; I was going to have casual sex and use a vibrator, and I was going to cum. I'd used a vibrator during sex before, with my long-term boyfriend, but even then, I could always tell he didn't really like it. At least in the beginning. When we were young, I think he saw it as a hassle or a blow to his ego. Over the years, it got much better but even then, I was always so sensitive about his reaction, their reactions. The way (weak) men think of vibrators as obstacles or competition has always irked me. That they even dare to have thoughts about how I reach my orgasm in a world that notoriously devalues and deprioritizes it enrages me. It's an act of revolution to cum as a woman, especially during casual sex. It's an act of rebellion to prioritize your own orgasm as a woman. That night, pulling out my vibrator in front of JP was an aberration. I took my own pleasure in my hands and for once I didn't check a man's face for validation. I wondered if JP had thought I was cumming back in the days of car-fucking. I wondered if now that he'd seen me really cum, how silly it seemed to ever think I had been cumming before. I didn't ask any follow-up questions. I didn't really need the answers.

Perhaps ironically, JP wasn't able to cum that night (because the condom was too tight). I didn't much care, if I'm being honest, not even a little. It seemed like the least he could do after all the times he'd gotten to cum and I had not. Honestly, he seemed unbothered by this and instead appeared mostly pleased by our chance to reconnect. We said our goodbyes, and I went back to studying and he went back to whatever he was doing with his life.

While I generally prefer not to give any man too much unearned credit, I often think about the role JP played in my sexual revolution. Being comfortable enough to bring out my vibrator was made possible because JP and I were a bridge between casual sex and something more familiar. JP had been one of my longest running booty calls of my life, so while there hadn't been many orgasms, there was a level of safety surrounding him.

I saw JP one more time after that night in my dorm-apartment. Four or five years later, after grad school and moving back to Vancouver, after dating around and waiting for a book deal, JP found me on Plenty of Fish—a happy surprise. JP was exactly what I needed in that moment—a little comfort, a little pleasure, a safe space with an old friend.

When I showed up at his doorstep for our date, he wrapped me up in his arms and practically swung me around. I used the bathroom, he poured himself a glass of wine, and we went out onto the balcony so I could smoke a joint. Things were going well at first, but it quickly became evident that perhaps he'd had a drink or two before I'd come over, which was fine, I guess. He didn't have anywhere else to be, but we all know how I feel about men getting sloppy. Instead of worrying about it (after all, that seemed like a him-problem not a me-problem), I proceeded to get super stoned. I figured I would just match his energy—everybody winning.

Standing close in that flirty way you do before anyone's made the first move, I asked him what he was doing for work these days. Instead of just answering (like a normal person), he gestured that we should go back inside his apartment, and he'd show me, which seemed extremely weird but like okay sure. How bad could it be? I ask you, dear reader, *how bad could it be?!?*

And that's when he pulled it out—it being literally the most delicious and amazing thing I'd ever seen.

I sat down on the couch, and he laid it on my lap.

I was practically drooling as he laid it across my thighs.

It, of course, was the most thorough and well stocked snack basket I'd ever seen. There was trail mix (the good kind with lots of chocolate), several varieties of chips, at least a dozen full-size chocolate bars plus an array of candy. Thinking we were about to make out though, I put the basket on the floor and turned to him—I may have been stoned but I still had my priorities straight. However, instead of kissing me, he reached down and pulled out an absolute monstrosity. If I gave you a million guesses, you would never guess what he wanted to show me. That man, the one I'd fucked in the backseat of a car during my youth and then later had been the co-pilot (or at least a ticketing agent) of my sexual revolution, was now standing before me drunk off wine trying to show me his...business presentation.

He wanted my opinion on the project, which should've been flattering but given our relationship and the fact that I was so high, I struggled to understand what was going on. JP tried to give me the whole presentation, flipping the pages and talking excitedly as he did. I tried not to cry (nor blink too intensely). Everything suddenly felt very, very wrong.

The truth was that his presentation was absolute trash, and it broke my heart for every second that he was giving it. That's the thing about empaths (aside from everybody thinking they are one), people always act like it's some kind of pleasant experience; it's not. I was sad for him. I was sad for me. I was sad for him because of me. The sadness was circular and everywhere. There was no way we could fuck now. Stoned out of my fucking mind, and essentially trapped until I could sober up enough to drive, I was stuck listening to a man who'd once been a hot booty call and was now just some corny dude drinking white wine and wasting my time.

After the "presentation", we watched sports center (possibly the same episode repeatedly?) for what felt like hours while I shoveled handfuls of trail mix down my gullet while sitting as far away as I could from him on the couch in mostly silence. Eventually I said my goodbye and practically ran down to my car (where I sat for another hour listening to a podcast because I wasn't quite ready to drive). He texted later that night to apologize for his allergies (which I guess is why he thought I'd left?). I responded that it was fine and never contacted him again. Whenever I think of JP, I try to remember the sexual revolution (and the trail mix—goddamn they were both delicious) and forget about the laminated nightmare (yes reader, the presentation was bound and laminated) that was his business presentation.

THE CHOSEN ONE

He said: *I haven't been honest with you* and then he crushed me like a bread truck or a freight train or the compounding interest on my student loan. It had all been a lie, but I wasn't surprised—the way I'm never surprised when the avocados on the countertop have gone off or the way it seems like everyone is probably just a little bit capable of murder.

    He said: *I'm married but there's a but to it* and then added: *if you care to hear it*. To which I said nothing and just watched as his WhatsApp status repeatedly changed from *online* to *typing*, and then back to *online* again. While he fumbled and made mistakes and tried to find the right words (there are no right words) I let him drown. I let the silence swallow him whole—his little bubbles of typing like last breaths. I paced my rage, the sense of betrayal, the feeling that I'd been fucked by a person I hadn't agreed to let fuck me. He was no longer who I had thought he was. He was a stranger, had always been a stranger, but was now stranger still. Moving further away with every statement he made, I waited, mostly silent and perched, until he opened the floodgates.

He said that his marriage had been open once. *Once*, I scoffed. He said that two and a half years ago it had all fallen apart. He said that he was sorry. I called him a monster and he promptly made it all about him. He told me that he was in tears over this, which seemed pathetic and greedy. I was the only one allowed to cry, and maybe his wife, though I had a distinct feeling he hadn't bothered to mention this to her.

I said, "You make me sick," and he said, "I'm puking my guts out over this." I didn't believe him and not because he had already lied about so much but because it seemed far too explosive a response. Yes, we had had *some kind* of connection. Yes, the chemistry (read: sex) was fun. But crying and puking over the possibility that I might hate him seemed too far-fetched. We'd both get over this—of that I was certain.

I called him a monster and he took all he hurt for himself. *My stomach* he complained *has been killing me all day*. He said it like his pain was for me. He made it seem like his body was attacking itself over the potential loss of me, but days later I would find out that he had an infection (one more fucking thing to worry about I guess). He said that he'd been broken up about this since the beginning. He had never lied to a woman about his situation before. Practically frothing at the mouth, I demanded to know why he hadn't told me from the beginning. I asked why he had lied to me from the start. I said *Why didn't you tell me before our first date, back when we were still just messaging?* Everything he typed after that was bullshit. The script for an outdated play called "all of our pathetic weakness" (and the reviews were already in—it was a flop, the critics panned it). He said that I was so sexy he couldn't bring himself to say it, which didn't even make sense except for when he added that he knew I wouldn't be okay with it, about which he was right. Though I don't know how he knew it so clearly. I wouldn't have fucked him, wouldn't have dated him, wouldn't have kissed him, if I had known he had a wife. Even if they were still in an open relationship, which it seemed both like they were and weren't, I still wouldn't have wanted him. It would have been easy for me to say no if he had told me that first night. I could've said no so easily back then.

Walking up to the restaurant that first night, I hadn't found him sexy. I had thought he seemed shorter than the 5'10" posted on his profile. He was dressed too casually, his body too comfortable; the hoody he wore, too beachy. Our first date was a catalog of flaws I brushed aside in favor of more positive attributes, the balance of which was still unclear in the end. He ate with his mouth open, talked with his mouth full, flagged down the waiter in a way that shocked me. When I asked him about it, he attributed it to his upbringing.

"In Israel it's not rude," he said, "That's just how we are."

The conversation flowed and he made me laugh, though I couldn't always tell if I was laughing with or at him. Open and talkative, he asked questions and made jokes. When the bill came and the waiter placed it on the table, we kept talking but by the time I had gone to the washroom and then returned, the bill had been taken care of. Three hours after we had been seated, they turned on the lights so we would leave. Looking back, a three-hour conversation seems pretty magical.

Now, he types so fast and at length, trying to explain away the logic of it all but the truth is that he didn't tell me that he was married because he's a selfish asshole. He wanted me and didn't want to risk not getting me. He lied because he's a piece of shit. I tell him that I hate him, that I feel disgusting, that I can't believe I ever let him touch me. It's all very dramatic, and I have no idea why I'm so upset by it—not really. My heart races but I don't cry, more anger than tears. More endless fucking disappointment. I know I'm being a jerk, and that I could just let him off the hook, I could just walk away, I won't be affected by this in the future. Even saying nothing seems a gentler option. But fuck him. I mean FUCK HIM. Because I have done nothing wrong (have I done anything wrong?). That's really why I say it. I feel like he's pulled me into this mess with him and for that I'm repulsed.

Weeks go by and I pull myself back together. Still, he's texting. I am entirely without empathy for him. I think about collecting on this debt he's incurred. I am damaged in a way that requires compensation. He had offered to take me out to dinner, practically begged, so that he could apologize to me. I thought about ordering appetizers and all the market price items. I planned to order dessert to go. I'd still order dessert while we were there. My fork perched to stab his hand should he try for a bite. He could get his own for all I cared. My just desserts. I deserved a piece of cake for finding out that a man I had briefly dated and vigorously fucked was married and had lied to my face. The fourth time he offered I accepted. He asked where I wanted to go, and I said I would get back to him (after I had figured out the most expensive place, I could think of that I wouldn't be embarrassed to be seen with him). I would go out to dinner and torture him with how good I looked and then I'd clean out his wallet out with lobster and cheesecake and I'd listen to his apology and never speak to him again.

Except never speaking to him again became, well maybe we could just be friends (except I didn't want to be friends). Never speaking to him again, very rapidly—way too rapidly— became acting exactly like we had been before except that now I knew he was married. Now I knew everything, which made me terrible and ashamed because I wanted him to choose me. Not in the lifetime way, not out of love, not even because I had anything against his wife (I didn't know her, in fact, I mostly just felt bad for her), but I wanted to be chosen. The words on a loop in my head, not yet uttered. "Would you get a hotel room if I asked?" If I said it, I would be the one pursuing this. I would be the one responsible for this. So, I said nothing.

I watch the text bubbles appear one after another after another and take pleasure in the fact that it seems like he's drowning. My rage is still mostly silent. It feels like he's my boyfriend and I've just found out that our whole relationship has been a lie. Except he's not my boyfriend. He's a man I've been on three dates with, three hangouts really. He's a man that I was dating, while still dating other people, and I sort of expected him to be dating other people (though not more than me, not better than me, definitely not more of a connection than we had). We had hung out three times, and then I got a cold, and he went to Israel and then I went on vacation. We had hung out three times and then spent three weeks barely texting and then three weeks of serious sexting and excitement. It was the last three weeks that bothered me the most. He could've saved me those three weeks and even the three weeks before that. He could've saved me so much time. That's the real betrayal. Six weeks of hope.

On our second date, I went over to his place to watch a movie. He lived in a townhouse and when I arrived the garage door and the door leading into the house were both open. He watched me park my car in his tiny driveway and then waddle and squeeze past all the things crowding the garage. The entranceway smelled like sweat, the way my gym clothes all start to smell the same, having spent prolonged periods of time in dampness. He had just moved in, so things were a little bit of a mess. In his office, on the first floor, he downloaded some movies for us to watch and gave me a selection to choose from. In the bathroom, there was no towel to dry my hands, so I had to use toilet paper and then there was no waste bin, so I had to flush twice. His bathroom was that of a bachelor, or a man cheating on his wife while she's still visiting family back in Israel.

I tried not to wonder about his wife. There was no point to that. Is she fat like me? Does her hair curl the way mine does? Is she funny or maybe she's boring? Is that why he wanted me? Because I was exactly the same or entirely different or some lonely caricature of middle ground.

My mother calls from California and I answer reluctantly. I know she can hear it in my voice. She doesn't say it but I'm not the same. The lump in my throat sticks to everything. "Dad says to make this quick because it's costing a fortune," she says to my relief. She has lost her wallet. She needs a picture of her passport. They are having eight different heart emojis of fun. "Do you want to talk," she asks but I say no and instead ask about the leaves she wanted me to rake up, about what I'm supposed to do with them once they're raked. I do not want to tell them that I have fucked a married man. I do not want them to know that I have been duped, that I am a fool made to dance too easily, that I was tricked with nothing but a slight of hand. I can't say the words that reveal how incredibly weak I am. The dam stretches and aches but does not break. She says, "We'll call again soon and—"

"No worries," I interrupt a little too quickly and then I hold my breath and hope she doesn't notice the depression seeping in.

"Okay then, talk soon. Love you."

"Love you."

I saw Ira one more time after that. I couldn't bring myself to spend a whole evening with him at a restaurant. I had seen who he was, and it wasn't for me. I had zero interest in carrying on anything further with him. But that doesn't mean I didn't still have revenge (and orgasms) in mind. A few weeks later, when I was feeling particularly horny, I texted Ira—want me to come over? He responded immediately *YES!*

Walking up to his bedroom, their bedroom, holding hands, I fed Ira a load of bullshit. I said that I had to leave by eleven because I had to be back home before midnight. It sounded like I was a teenager trying to get home before her parents knew she was out with a boy, which in the weirdest way I was. I told him that I had to be home before midnight because if I wasn't I'd have to explain to my parents that I hadn't been out at a coffeeshop writing. I didn't want to explain what I was really doing. I said it like that was reasonable and not that I was a woman in her late thirties who could do whatever the fuck she wanted. Still though, going out that night, I'd told my parents (who ask out of curiosity not concern) that I was going to my favorite late night coffee shop to write.

I don't think Ira paid much attention. I don't think he thought I was that serious, and of course I wasn't except for one small thing. Ira and I messed around for a little bit before I asked him to go down on me. I had set the alarm on my phone for eleven. I had wanted to have a hard out just in case I couldn't find the words to be a villain in the moment. I'm still not totally sure what pushed me over the edge, whether it was the sound of my alarm or Ira's skill at eating pussy, but I came hard to the sound of my alarm going off.

Ira lay back on the bed, extremely proud of himself, but tonight there would be no post-game cuddling. Tonight, there would be no returning of the favor. I got up from the bed and went into the ensuite bathroom. I could hear him asking through the door, "Do you really have to go?" and then following my silence, "You can stay a bit longer, can't you?" I used his hand towel to wipe all the sweat from my body and his saliva from my pussy. I thought about hanging it up on the rack, but I didn't want his wife to suffer, just Ira. She hadn't done anything wrong. I could hear him trying to convince me through the door. I looked at my face in the mirror, and realized that I could, in fact, be a total asshole (to someone who deserved it). I slid the door open, tossed my sweaty towel to Ira and walked around the bed looking for my shirt.

"I can't," I lied without even the tiniest hint of remorse. Or maybe it wasn't a lie. I was lying about my ability to stay later but not my ability to stay at all. I didn't have it in me to give him any reward or pleasure—he deserved nothing. The clock had struck midnight (or eleven, as it were) and my carriage was waiting. I shrugged my shoulders with a guilt I didn't feel.

"You can," he begged. I explained that I couldn't, fed him more bullshit, grabbed my purse, and left. Driving home that night was electric. I don't know what had me more juiced up—the incredible orgasm I'd just enjoyed or the plate of revenge I'd just served. It didn't much matter, I guess. The result was the same. Joy and pleasure oozed from my pores and for perhaps the first time in my life I had taught a man a lesson he wouldn't soon forget.

KNOWING ABOUT FAT GIRLS

He is everything I dislike about her (which is hard to admit about a friend, who's now an ex-friend, and which should make it easier to admit but doesn't). The ending wasn't dramatic; things simply fizzled out, more a loss of touch than crimes of friendship. But still, it's a hard thing to admit you carried around a list about someone. Not a literal list, just a tallying of irritants and slights tucked up under your ribs. A thing mostly ignored except for a gentle poking during the rough times. I'm not sure what's harder to admit—that I disliked so many things about her or that I continued the friendship anyway, until I didn't. Sometimes I wonder if they were soul mates, the way the seemed the same in all the worst ways. I shrug the feeling off because I'm sure people have lists about me. Long, extensive lists about my drawbacks and annoying idiosyncrasies—the way I talk about men, my voice too loud, my laugh too certain.

A few weeks after being back in Vancouver, I went to a party at my friend's loft apartment. Standing around her kitchen island, in the kind of apartment I'd never be able to afford, I was involved in a heated discussion. I was talking (lecturing) three men about how disgusting it was the way men pressure women beyond their sexual boundaries when this girl stood up from the couch behind us and said, "But you're taking away women's agency," and just like that I let her have mine.

She seemed to think women couldn't be pressured into sexual acts because we can say no and mean it and end things just like that, and I got confused about my point because of course that was the ideal scenario but here, right in front of me, at this party of lawyers and art directors and bartenders, stood three men who had, only moments before, said that when a woman said no to sex, that it was okay, standard even, to try and convince her. And hadn't I been convinced and cajoled and pressured and forced and turned my head away and *maybe this is what I want* because I am a sex-positive woman and what am I waiting for anyway it's not like this could possibly change the way he sees me, we're all enlightened here, right?

The men at the party said that women didn't always know what they wanted, especially when it came to sex, and then one of them made a comparison between sex and cereal. This full-grown adult man stood in front of me at this party with a face full of absolute sincerity and gave the following example:

He said, "Like, if I offered a woman a bowl of cereal and she said no, but then I was like, hey wait, this cereal might be really good, you've never tried this cereal before, how do you even know you don't want it?"

He said that's what it was like to talk to a woman, to try to convince her to have sex with you and all the others nodded in agreement. But I couldn't understand his point because I've never not known if I wanted cereal shoved into my body.

My friend, a lawyer, a feminist, *my friend* leaned over and said, "Because not every girl" and then she nodded in my direction as if to say that not every girl was like me, and I'm not sure if she made the jerk-off motion or that's just what it felt like but that's what she meant. She meant that not everyone gives a handjob to get out of a situation where they've said no to sex and the man they're with doesn't listen, and I went from zero to deserved it before my heart had a chance to skip a beating. Looking back now, I guess it wasn't so much the list that ended our friendship. I didn't storm out of the party; I didn't even really say anything to her about it. But the feeling that she sided with the cereal rapists was a step too far, a belief too unbearable, a taste too sour in my mouth.

Even through my resentment of what had happened at that party, I was jealous of both of them—my friend who's no longer a friend and that woman from the couch. I wanted to have the same life those women had. I wanted to be someone who had never experienced pressure from men, and more than that I wanted to be a woman who had never caved under the pressure from men. I wondered what their dating lives must be like. My entire dating life can be described in terms of men who don't listen. Men who ask for pictures when I've said no. Men who push for sex when I've said kissing was enough. Men who are only vaguely interested until I've said that we're done and then "maybe...," they say, jamming their foot into the door I'm trying to close. I wrap my fingers around their soles to push them away. I say no, I say go slow, I say the door is closed you missed your shot, and they say, "Maybe, we'll see," like I'm a ghost or a child or a woman.

Because we're not friends anymore, when I match on Tinder with Elias, who I recognize as someone my ex-friend dated a few times, I don't unmatch. She had told me once that he was an amazing lover, which made it even harder to believe they hadn't worked out as a couple. They were both intelligent and socially aware while simultaneously lacking self-awareness to a shocking degree. Pretentiousness dripped from their pores. They both seemed completely shocked over their dating debacles (which isn't the same struggle as me, to be clear). I know that I date fools, that I fuck selfish men I will regret letting touch me, that I take risks where risks are perhaps unnecessary. I am (mostly) entirely aware of all the mistakes and missteps I make, even if only in hindsight. I'm also acutely aware of how they're both conventionally attractive and I am not. Many of my dating choices are made because of this awareness. Neither of them has to make such concessions.

Standing in Elias' apartment, I make a joke about the milkshakes he had promised were the world's best, the ones he had texted about as if that was a reason I would agree to come over to his apartment. I look at the two glasses, mostly drunk, sitting on the counter and ask, "Where's mine?" even though I don't want one. He doesn't laugh—he doesn't even crack a smile. The way men aren't taught about social graces always shocks me—robots without a clue. The irony of women spending our whole lives being told to smile when it's men who have cement faces. In his kitchen, Elias awkwardly begins to list the ingredients of the already drunk milkshakes, "Blueberries, ice cream…" as if I had never had one before. This is not a hit-cook-show but somehow, he is so fucking proud. I find it embarrassing and move to the couch in the hopes that he'll relax and become more interesting.

Our conversation on the app was paragraph-good right from the start. Huge bubbles of text sent back and forth across Tinder while we got to know each other through fully formed sentences. He asked questions, I asked questions—we were already a well-oiled machine. Then one night I went to a poetry reading by myself and it turned out it was within 3km of his apartment. When he noticed, he messaged immediately to invite me over.

Message me when you're here he typed, *and we can go for a walk around the block or something.*

Both ridiculous and perfectly logical, the walk was a return policy—we were keeping the tags on just in case one of us was a total nut job or didn't look like our pictures, and by the time we made it back to the front of his building, we could decide if we wanted a refund. Yes, admittedly it would be brutal if either of us was unsatisfied with the merchandise and had to actually verbalize it, but less so than if we had to spend several hours with someone who later admitted the shirt hadn't fit right from the get-go. I was not an ill-fitting garment (or, if I was, at the very least, I didn't want to be worn out of the store).

Everyone thinks I'm so judgmental and hard on men, but what they don't consider is how many gut reactions and instincts I let slide because of a misguided belief and naïve optimism that people might just surprise you. People are rarely surprising. By the time I'm judging a man, I've let a hundred missteps pass by without comment. Men have no idea the free passes they're given in life.

Elias was wearing pants that tapered at the ankles the first time I saw him. He was the same height as me and wearing tapered olive-green pants, which I bet some other girl would love, lots of girls even, but not me and not on him. He immediately walked way too fast, which I initially misread as dissatisfaction and later recognized as a lack of consideration. He said he walked so fast because that's how he walked to work, in a hurried rush, which seemed like a terrible way to live. Social awareness would tell you to slow down. Common sense should facilitate the idea that we were not in a hurry and that he should be accommodating and normal and on his best behavior (putting a slower foot forward). Eventually I had to joke around and pretend to jog just so he would get the idea. I was ready to get back in my car by the time we made it back to the front door.

He said, "Get on your knees and face away from me." He said it like it was a totally normal request and not something that sounded incredibly cringe and probably straight out of some *Shades of Grey* nonsense. He said it like he was about to perform some wild sex act that certainly—most definitely—without doubt—would blow my fucking mind.

He said, "Take your dress off," but I didn't want to take my dress off. I had my usual first date armor on—tights up to my bra, full-brief panties on, unshaven legs. I hadn't known I'd be meeting up with a guy tonight. I wasn't hook up ready. Or maybe none of that shit mattered and the real point was that I didn't want to get naked in front of him, yet. I'm not even totally sure I wanted to be there at all.

Earlier on the couch he had said he liked things to be equal in a sexual relationship, which sounded fair enough, and then added that, "The woman should be submissive sometimes and aggressive other times." I was nodding my head yes while thinking, *uh I don't know about that, man.* At the time, I thought the issue was that I like the man to be the aggressor but that wasn't really true. I mean shit, I have this entire move where I pull back from a kiss about three times before I let them really kiss me just to tease it out, just to be the one in control. What I didn't like was the way he used the word *should.* Like he had all these ideas about how a woman should (and shouldn't) act and suddenly I was expected to be a part of that.

Elias had fucked my friend. I think. I know they'd gone out and that she'd raved about what a good lover he was and now (since we weren't really friends anymore), I guess it was okay to give him a shot. I have to admit that I'm not sure what my interest in him was (or even if there *was* any interest). He wasn't cool. He wasn't fun. He was exactly like my friend who was no longer my friend, and none of the ways they were similar impressed me. I think I was holding on to the person I had thought he was while we had been messaging and everything since had just been accidental missteps that surely weren't an indication of his genuine personality. That and my ex-friend had painted him as this amazing lover and *who am I not to indulge?*

My uncertain interest wasn't the only hurdle. There was also the ever-present issue of my fatness and whether or not that would factor into the experience. As always, I hoped it wouldn't. But the biggest difference between my ex-friend and I (personalities aside) was that she wasn't fat, and I was absolutely fat, and I wasn't sure

Elias had ever been with a fat girl before. While I don't like men who fetishize fat women, I like a man who's been with at least a few of us before. I like a man who knows about apron bellies and rolls and fat in places other women might not have so much fat. I like a man who knows that just because I'm wearing a dress, doesn't mean that there isn't a belly underneath. I wasn't hiding anything, but still, men are notoriously stupid and likely to turn that stupidity into rage when found out. I wasn't hiding anything, but I didn't know if he knew I was fat, understood I was fat. I had a bad feeling.

Needless to say, climbing down onto his bed, which was really just a mattress on the floor (shocking only because his apartment itself screamed that he had money), I was nervous that my fatness would come as a surprise. Admittedly, it's weird to be worried about being judged for your body by a man without a bedframe, but that's what it's like being a fat woman. Even when you're the most confident, even when you're the most self-assured, you never know when you're going to have a bad night. And you'll never really know how bad it'll be until it happens. And even then, you'll never really know for sure.

But, with Elias, I know *for sure*. Elias didn't know about bellies. Elias didn't know about fat girls. Looking back (and if I'm being honest, probably even in the moment), I knew I shouldn't have extended the sexual opportunity to him, but I did and for that I will always be sorry. Am I sorry I hooked up with a guy who may have meant something to a friend who once meant something to me? Yes, and no. I was mostly just sorry that this man had gotten the chance to even been in the presence of either of us let alone allowed to touch and explore our bodies. She didn't know about this night, so there was no hurt to feel bad over. Plus, I was tired of always being the good friend. We hadn't spoken in years. Our friendship was dead. I could fuck Elias. But I wouldn't fuck Elias. Thank God I never fucked Elias.

I got naked with Elias, sort of, and then things suddenly got real weird, real quick. After much prodding and cajoling from him to take off my clothing, I'd gone to the bathroom and taken my tights and panties off. I don't remember if it was when he touched my belly, whether it hung too low, or if his short t-rex arms couldn't reach my pussy but the tempo of our kissing quickly changed. I don't quite know how to explain it because it was just a feeling—but it's a feeling every fat girl knows. It's fast and sharp, a slap in the face with no culprit ready to admit their violence. One second, we were making out and he was trying to get it and the next was deafening silence. I went to the bathroom and put my panties and tights back on.

At the front door, he kissed me passionately and for way too long (which was perhaps the weirdest part given how he'd just behaved). I had deleted his number by the time I got to my car, not that it mattered anyway because I never heard from him again. The irony is that I wasn't hurt that he didn't like my body. I was done caring what men thought. I was irritated that he'd put me in this position, that he'd invited me over when he didn't know about fat girls, that I'd entertained his boring conversation and let him touch me when he didn't know about fat girls.

It's very easy not to make people feel like trash, and I was so goddamn tired of men who hadn't the skill not to crush people. I was so tired of men with the audacity to act so callously. I was so tired of men like Elias. But just as tired as I was, I was equally capable of moving on. Beyond this story here, I never think of Elias. I've barely given him a second thought outside of these words here. Elias wasn't worth my time (and he wasn't worth my friend's time either—though I'm never not sad when I think about how she had said what a great lover he was—what terrible fucking she must be used to).

I wouldn't be surprised if Elias was married with kids by now because that's the world we live in. Men are never held accountable for the way they've treated women in the past. That's actually one of the things I find hardest to believe whenever I hear about someone getting married—the way women never ask about a man's past in the ways that matter. Women always ask who a man is still attached to, who they need to worry about, who else he might be fucking—but I've never met another woman who would ask a man whom he fucked over, to whom he was cruelest, the biggest and harshest mistakes he's made at the expense of a woman, which women he's damaged with his words and his actions. I've never met a man who's been held accountable. Which is a wild thing. Not that I'm really faulting Elias for disliking an apron belly. Fat bodies aren't for everybody and that's a choice you get to make (though you should absolutely look at how and why that came to be because baby, preferences are not inherent, they are ingrained). But don't get a fat girl naked if you're afraid of her body.

GIRLS JUST WANNA HAVE DESSERT

When I first started dating, I thought my options were limited because I was fat, and in that there is definitely some truth worth unpacking. The world treats fat people terribly. But as far as being treated badly by men, that appeared to be universal. Every time I would find myself unable to match with anyone interesting, unable to get a second or third or fourth date, unable to get a man to see me as anything other than something to fuck—I would talk to other women about dating. Sure enough, there results (and struggles) were virtually the same. Thin women get treated terribly. Thin women get cheated on and objectified. Thin women are abused and mistreated and mislead. Thin women are just as miserable. Thin women don't get many (if any) orgasms from casual sex. Which isn't to say that fatphobia isn't real—fatphobia in dating is as real as it gets. But when you're down in the dumps thinking that dating is a nightmare because you're [insert marginalization], you can rest assured that it's actually because straight men are terrible. But again, I didn't always feel this way.

There was a time I really thought it was because I was fat that I couldn't get a man to see me as a human being. As a fat woman, I couldn't get men to stop wanting to fuck my body (my body, my body, but never me). As a woman, I was just a jar of doll parts to them. They all wanted to unscrew the lid and stick their dick in. An adventure, one would call it. Another said, "I've never been with a big girl before." The next would add, "I want to fuck an older woman like you," and they must have heard him across all the waters of earth because after that they all started to say it that way. A fat woman. An older woman. So fixed and fascinated on it. I was a car accident or a bank robbery or a murder scene. They wanted a taste; they wanted to dip their finger in my blood and smear it across their lips. They wanted a little tragedy in their life. They want a prize for their kill.

But who was to blame? Someone had to be to blame. Someone had to be responsible. To have so many men—not just one broken solider but an entire army—behave this way. I couldn't help but think about what a terrible job their parents had done. They want to fuck up when I was always fucking down. They were somewhere between duds and monsters and my only options.

Advice from people about dating comes in two forms and two forms only. It's both that I need to be more open and give guys a chance. This advice comes from people who've apparently never met men because they think I should be a much better judge of character, only willing to date age-appropriate, incredibly intelligent men whose social awareness probably needs some tuning but who are generally good people (this advice comes from women who've spent their lives shrinking for men).

That's a whole lot to balance and know in advance, and honestly, it's a lot to be able to find in the first place. The older I get the more I realize how few and far between intelligent men are. It's hard to be open but selective and know people before you've gotten to know them. So, I cast a wide net and regularly get lost at sea.

I say, "he rejected me."

I say, "we only went out twice."

I say, "he was too young, but…"

They answer, "he was probably intimidated by you," and I can't help but think *I wish* knowing it could never be true. Men have no concept of their own (lack of) value and so being intimidated by anything other than beauty is something I've yet to witness in real life.

Someone asks, "Did you even like him?" and the answer is sadder than you'd expect because probably not. I say this not because I'm hurt, or defensive, but because it's the truth. I rarely date men I actually like, they're simply not in my pool of fish. I don't know where the witty, intelligent men are but very few of them like fat women.

Did I even like him? I wonder after every rejection. Maybe I just liked the idea of him. Maybe I liked who I was in his gaze. This pain is a pain I need heard. To not have my tears fall on deaf ears, but things have gone silent, so I have stopped crying in public. I cannot let my heart be tended in this way, so it becomes untenable.

My thesis advisor wrote in the margins of one of my drafts: *Tell me how he looks, describe how attractive he is. Don't just say that he was too good looking.* But I don't because my attraction is not your attraction. The point isn't that his hair was soft, it was that I had wanted to touch it. The facts are not important. What matters is that when I say he was too good looking for me, you feel it. You imagine someone out of your league in whatever ways you've always felt just a little bit less than. The point is to push your fingers into the soft spots, the places where bruises exist too far under the surface to be visible. The point is the discomfort and then the relief. The point isn't to travel far away from yourself, it's to look inward. The goal is to press my heart against yours and feel just a little bit less alone. Or maybe I don't know anything at all. My characters do not have faces because, after all, they are not characters but memories. The faces have faded, a mirage is all that's left.

Every so often, when dating is at its worst or some particular man has disappointed me in some unique and jarring way, I wonder why I continue. I ask myself why. To the eyes of an unfaithful observer, at least on the surface, it seems that men are entrenched in my veins, wrapped tightly around my heart like ivy or arteries. All my life I would've expected to be stronger by this point. This heart wasn't built for attacks.

When I start to feel this way—like my heart is on the outside, my skin raw and crawling, like I've become hollow giving everything away to men, I remember that I should take more breaks from dating. I should focus on myself and nothing else. I shouldn't expect anything from men so that they never disappoint me. Not every lesson can be learned in a day (or a decade). Logic can only get you so far when your heart refuses to show it the map.

Ignacio and I meet through Tinder and after an appropriate number of messages, I suggest he adds me on facebook. I didn't used to think adding someone on facebook was a good idea. Now, though, now I'm tired of all the ways men risk nothing and women risk everything to date. I know most people aren't as public and open as I am, but I need to anchor him with something. I'm tired of finding out a man is not for me (read: a total loser) after meeting. I want to save myself the hassle and the time. I want things to be easy for once. But he says *no* almost immediately. *Facebook is only for friends and family.*

I understand in so much as that's his right to have a boundary for himself. Nonetheless, my interest is immediately lost. He wants me to risk potential death (or possibly some mild awkwardness) to go on a date with him without risking anything himself? Hard pass. I don't unmatch, but I stop answering (quickly). I stop answering questions (enthusiastically) and no longer ask him any of my own. I'm not sure he ever really notices. He misreads my "hardly interested" as "hard to get". We spend the next four months—which is not a typo and instead both an insane and completely factual amount of time—locked in a battle of apathetic (on my part) and unaware (on his part) messaging. Long after I actually think we'll ever go out; he shows up in my *People You Might Know* on Facebook and I add him because why not—what's the worst that can happen at this point. He accepts almost instantly.

For four months he had messaged me. He asked how I'm doing. He made mindless small talk, always polite and kind but never intriguing. He didn't ask anything big. There are no, "What makes you happiest in life?" Or, "How important do you think blank is?" type questions. The conversation never really went anywhere. He asked me out more than once but did it in a way that makes it so easy to refuse. He says that he *thinks* he'll be free on Friday night, and I latch on like a leech. *You think?* I type. *Judgmental smirk face emoji. Cut the shit emoji. You're a grown-up emoji. Knife knife gun gun gun why don't you know how to make a plan emoji.*

He said something about being on call for work. He said something that could be legitimate, would be legitimate if it wasn't for all the people who have ever bailed on a party because they were "sick" or cancelled plans because they got "called into work" or stood you up for a date because they had to "clean up a murder" or whatever. Those people have ruined it for everyone because there's no way to tell if an excuse is real. There's no way to tell if you're being compassionate and understanding or a pushover. And because I am no pushover, I told him no. I said that I am unwilling to make plans with someone who clearly struggles to make plans. I said that I am not willing to put my life on hold for his possibilities (or something slightly less dramatic). He stops asking for the night but not for good. He asked me out another time and I say no.

One day he messages to say that he wishes he could hang out but is so busy working.

I say *meh*.

I say *you're acting as if I had asked you out and I have not*.

He says *I like how feisty you are*.

Men are always confusing a lack of interest with a challenge worth undertaking. Men are always making it more difficult on themselves, using time instead of their own value as a way to win me over. There is no need to chip away at woman if you're worth something. You can just show them, right from the beginning—you can just be your best self. There's this saying that men love the chase, like it's a biological imperative or something but so is murdering your competition, and I think it's safe to say we (should've) evolved past that. I just wanted a man to recognize that I was fantastic, right from the start. I was tired of trying to convince men that I was amazing.

But the messages just kept coming, and I mostly resented their presence. Except for one night, when he asks how I am, and because I'm a messy bitch, I answer truthfully that I'm in a horrible mood. He asks why and I tell him that I've been dumped (or maybe I said rejected, which would've been far more accurate). He says all the right things (in theory) about how he wants to take me out, how he wants to show me a good time (no euphemism). How he wants to treat me wonderfully, which is exactly what I deserve (his words not mine). He says all the things that make it sound like he thinks I'm worth something. He suggests we go out for a meal. He wants to make me feel special. He wants to treat me well. He wants me to have food.

A few weeks later we meet for tacos in Gastown. Everything is delicious and perfect except the place we're at doesn't have dessert, which is too bad because "I really love a churro."

"I know where we can go," he says confidently, and he takes me to another bar down the street. When we arrive and there's only one seat at the bar available, he insists I take it. He gets a drink and I get a diet coke and then he places an order for churros with dulce de leche. They bring it in a to-go container when we've finished our drinks and he hands it to me.

"You want one?" I ask, but he pushes the container back towards me with a smile on his face, "No, they're for you." He pays the bill, and we go back to his apartment because apparently my fetish is men caring enough about me as a human to want me to feed me, to make me happy. It's really that simple. Which always makes me wonder why men struggle so much. One to-go order of churros and I was smitten (at least for the next few hours until the spell wears off). Churros are delicious, after all, but they're not magic.

Ignacio and I never fuck, and I love that for me. His name is Ignacio which I learn is shortened to Nacho which only becomes funnier and more brilliant when you know that my online persona is Victoria Nachos, and we went for tacos on our first date. Two Nachos eating Tacos—the poetry writes itself.

Ignacio lives downtown in the smallest studio I've ever seen (which I say without judgement having mostly lived in studio apartments throughout my adult life). I can barely bring myself to pee because I'm certain he'll hear every little sprinkle. There's no need for an apartment tour—there are two bar stools beneath the countertop and nowhere else to sit. That's the whole tour. He pulls a murphy bed down from the wall and we lay on it (because there's no room for a couch) to watch Netflix. Three hours later, we have made out through multiple episodes of *Making a Murderer*. I keep asking him to restart it during the little breaks we take to catch our breath. "We missed the beginning," I say laughing.

"You don't need to see it," he says pulling me close, and again we are all lips and tongues and hungry roaming hands. I can feel the panting in both our chests. Even though I have zero intention of fucking Ignacio, at least not tonight, I am thoroughly enjoying the hook up.

Ignacio and I never hang out again but it's hardly worth being sad over. Given how long it had taken to be able to put a first date together, I had little expectation for a second. Hence, why I hadn't slept with him. For one of the very times in my life, I didn't go into a first date with the hope of a second. I took the night for exactly what it was—churros and kissing and laughs. A good time had by all. I still think about Ignacio every so often (usually when

I've scrolled all the way through my Netflix *continue watching* queue to see *Making a Murderer* there at the end of the row).

BEAUTY FADES BUT RED FLAGS ARE FOREVER

Fayez looks like Joe Manganiello (True Blood era). We meet in the summer and eat plates of tapas at a place on main where the front wall is just one big open window. The breeze keeps the sweat on my brow at bay. We laugh with each other as the restaurant fills, empties, fills, and empties again. He pays and we go for a walk around the block. Fayez towers over me and I wonder if the good smell is deodorant or cologne. Twenty steps away from being back at my car, Fayez pulls me into an embrace. We kiss long and slow against a cement wall hidden from onlookers. I float home.

On our second date we go for coffee, and he invites his friend. He wants me to meet his friends. He wants to show me off. This is an aberration when you're a fat woman dating. The ease with which a fat girl forgets her common sense is like butter on hot corn. Your entire life is spent being hidden, watching the face of others checking for the look of shame, not always and not with everyone but often enough that you know to look. Even if you never tolerated it. Even if you always ended things the second you felt hidden. None of that heals the wound. None of that makes you forget. So, when a man invites his friend to come meet you, when a man wants to show you off early and with intention, you melt into every wound you've ever had. You do not recognize the red flag. You are too close to it. You are too blinded by the hurts of your past.

By the end of the date, meeting Fayez's friend didn't seem that weird. They talked about soccer, and we all made jokes. His friend asked me lots of questions and made far more conversation than Fayez did, in a cute way. By the time his friend left, I couldn't help but wonder if I now had a crush on both of them. When they both asked me to come watch them play soccer, I assured them I would (already thinking of all the fantasies I was about to have about them).

After that second date, Fayez and I went back to his place and things started to lose their sheen, just a little. His house was empty when we arrived, by which I mean both that there was no one else there and also that within the walls of his room there was virtually no furniture. Now look here, dear reader, when I say that I have empathy for anyone experiencing financial scarcity, I really mean it. As a grown adult living back in my childhood bedroom with the hopes of gaining traction in my writing career, I know what it is to not have much to your name. The issue wasn't that Fayez was living sparsely, the issue was that it was a surprise. Which, I guess, is a pretty hard thing to avoid. No one wants to hear about how you've barely got two nickels to rub together on a first date.

More than just a sign of his financial insecurity, his lack of bedframe made me question things he'd said on our first date. As it turns out, "working for a moving company" was more like "helping a friend move for pizza and beer." I pulled at the threads of what he'd told me so far. As it turns out, he was only very recently separated. The story unraveled further when he told me that he had emigrated for a woman who lived up north. Perhaps unsurprisingly, he quickly realized how cold it was up north and also that they didn't love each other anymore and I got the feeling he'd come all the way here from Tunisia for a sugar mamma. The irony of my financial situation made the whole thing seem laughable. But then again, maybe I was being too sensitive, too jaded, too quick to assume the worst. I tucked my concerns in my pockets for later. Fayez put on a movie, and we messed around (fully clothed, because ya'll know I've stopped fucking on first dates). Did I mention he looked like fucking Joe Manganiello?!

After messing around, he walked me past his roommate in the living room and out to my car. His roommate was pushing sixty and eating a tv dinner. Why were all the young men I kept dating living with old men? Fayez held my hand, and I avoided making eye contact with his red flag.

Outside, he kissed me in the middle of the road. He didn't want to let me go. The way the smallest amount of effort feeds you when you've been starved for so long. But that doesn't mean I didn't see the red flags from the start. I've never understood the way some people pretend not to have seen all the signs in hindsight.

I once (briefly) dated a married man who pretended to be sent off to war during the whole weapons of mass destruction bs. It turns out his wife had just returned after an extended vacation in North Carolina visiting family. Now, to be clear, I didn't think he'd had a wife. That wasn't the flag I ignored. But there were flags. One time, I asked him what time it was for him (you know, over there, in "Iraq"), and the answer he gave had an eleven-hour time difference. I asked another time, and this time he answered with a different time difference. I didn't call him on it. I was maybe twenty years old, and I was busy having fun out at nightclubs and with other boys. So, while I didn't know he was cheating on his wife (for the third time as I would soon find out), I without a doubt saw that red flag and waved it on by. There were a few of them, always related to dishonesty. I noted them and then promptly ignored them. I was young and dumb and had nothing on the line. But I can still admit they were there. I don't understand the point of pretending they're not there. *How do you learn if you can't admit your mistakes?*

I saw Fayez's red flags from the jump (or from a little bit after the jump, I guess the timeline doesn't really matter). I was prepared for them long before they came to light. He was dropping hints like Hansel and Gretel. And yet still, I kept going out with him (BECAUSE HE LOOKED LIKE JOE MANGANIELLO! And I was having fun).

As a society, I think we've really downplayed how attraction affects straight women. We act like women always need an emotional connection (false!) to enjoy casual sex but people rarely discuss the nuance of that. Do you need that emotional connection to feel safe? To cum? To enjoy yourself? What if, and hear me out, men weren't absolute fucking nightmares poised to treat you like shit the second they've gotten what they wanted from you—could that be the reason you need an emotional connection? Because a man being emotionally connected to you gives a higher guarantee he won't hurt you and the safety of not getting hurt is what you need to enjoy sex. I don't have all the answers but at the very least, I'm kind of begging everyone to think about it. Because I've said it before and I'll say it again—I don't need an emotional connection to have sex and I definitely don't need it to cum, but I do need something to make fucking a stranger safe enough to be fun. Physical safety. Emotional safety. The safety to let go. So please stop perpetrating gendered nonsense if you don't at least have some nuanced thoughts and varied anecdotal evidence.

Just as enjoyment of casual sex is gendered (because of the orgasm gap), wanting to fuck based on attraction alone is also very gendered and that too is false. Joe Manganiello (real or look alike) is hot enough to just fuck. I've said before that most men aren't hot enough to attract me without having a good personality, but here's the thing—that's because most men aren't very hot. If that makes me sound like an asshole, or makes you want to ask: okay but aren't you someone who falls outside of the beauty standard? To that, I would say yes, and that's why I've worked my whole life to be accomplished and funny, introspective, wise, kind and interesting, a good conversationalist, a phenomenal lover. And even then, I'd urge you to see that men do, in fact, find me very attractive (regardless of whether or not they want to date me, men are regularly and without fail attracted to me). All I'm saying is that maybe it's not gender fucking up casual sex for all of us—because women do fuck because of attraction, and we do fuck because of desire, and the fact that so few of us want to fuck you casually has more to do with your performance and appearance than anything related to be *the fairer sex*.

On our third date, Fayez and I fucked on his floor mattress where I had forgotten the cardinal rule about hot people—most of them are terrible at sex. What can I say, I'm forever an idiot-optimist. The sex wasn't bad, but it was neutral, a thing that becomes a disappointment simply because you had expected it to be better. But it had been fun (though obviously I did not cum because he was young and clueless, and I didn't have a vibrator handy). We fucked with his taught body pressed against mine, his silver cross dangling close enough to my mouth that I could eat it. After he finished (and the sex was over, apparently), he had a smoke and then said he wanted to take me for Tunisian food. I agreed because of how he said it, how he wanted to show me his culture, his people's food. Looking back now, I was blinded by the dessert with Ignacio. I took the gesture as a sign of care instead of just a sign that he was hungry.

At the restaurant, I ordered a chicken dish (the cheapest option though it still had a price tag of $36). He ordered something similar along with a glass of wine. When the bill came, I knew instantly that I wouldn't be seeing him again. He paid for his half and then handed me the merchant terminal. There was nothing else to do except pay for my own meal (which for those keeping track was an expensive meal at a restaurant I hadn't chosen). Over the course of the meal, he also talked about his ex a lot and it became overwhelmingly clear that he didn't want to be in a relationship with a woman so much as her bank account. Which is like, go on with your bad self-babe, get that bag. But not from me, and not just because I had no bag of my own to give. Plus, even if I had the money to spare, the idea that I'd give it to a man who hadn't even made me cum was wild. Even if he looked like Joe Manganiello. Beauty is cool for a while, but it gets boring quick (real quick).

I dropped Fayez off that night back at his place. I didn't go inside. I didn't text him again. We both knew it was over.

THE PERFECT "NO"

Sexual liberation doesn't happen overnight. You don't develop self-esteem in one sitting. We aren't made for perfection.

The first time I fuck someone before I really want to, I don't recognize it for what it is right away. You can think and think and think and still not have any answers. Over time, though, if you keep at it, it'll come to you. But it doesn't happen overnight. You don't become the woman you were meant to be from the beginning. Unless you're lucky, and I'm not sure I've ever met someone that was lucky.

It took me a long time to understand that I had a scarcity mentality because I was a fat woman (and not fat in that socially acceptable coke bottle body way). I was an apron belly fat woman with a deep-seated feeling that there was undeniably an end limit on the number of possible dates I could have. There would come a time when Vancouver would simply run out of men interested in me, and so I had to ignore the red flags (at least partially) and I had to convince myself I wanted them more than I did (amping them up in my mind in ways they themselves would never be capable of delivering on). Every man I'd ever given a handjob to instead of fucking, every man I'd ever fucked instead of just leaving, every man I hadn't murdered after fucking me and not making me cum—those men all remained in my life (and between my thighs) longer than they deserved because of scarcity.

The change didn't happen overnight. After all, I'd spent my whole life knowing my value as a person, as a human. What I didn't know (how the fuck could I not know?) was that I could do whatever I wanted with my body. I know that sounds silly, reading it in this book about fucking and feminism, that it took till I was in my late thirties to know that I could say no and limit access to my body and still there would always be another chance to date a mediocre dude and fuck an unbelievably hot one. Perhaps the most important lesson I taught myself was that I could change the course of any sexual activity and I could do it at any time. I didn't have to go through with anything I didn't want to. I didn't have to put in effort to preserve men—the good men would take my no and wait for further direction.

Peter and I go for sushi off campus. He's in town for business at the university. He's age appropriate (older than me in fact) with a grown-up job. We discuss dating and politics and the vibe of different cities. He's tall and bald and after dinner (which he pays for) we walk around Kits. Together we drive back to UBC where he's staying for the duration of the conference. He doesn't like the rap music I have playing, and I put something more soothing on for him. I think he's staying in a hotel until he directs me to the college dorms, the ones I remember from first and second year. He leads me inside, down the long hallway smelling slightly of beer and teenage boys, and then into his tiny little single bed dorm room which I guess is fine and fun and cute but is kind of a boner killer. We makeout for a while and I try not to fall off the bed. After I've enjoyed myself enough, I leave because I don't want to fuck. That's a fun new thing I'm trying.

He probably thought we would fuck (and maybe I did too). Maybe it's because he's only in town for a day or two or maybe it's because the dorm room bummed me out or maybe it's just because I didn't want to—but we don't fuck. I don't give him a participation trophy handjob. I don't need to keep him hanging on. That is no longer my job. I don't need to balance the chemistry and interest with not desiring a relationship. I don't have to explain myself to anyone. I want to go and so I go. He has a boner, and I don't fucking care and it's not because he did anything wrong (honestly, he was lovely), and it's not because he wasn't someone I might want to fuck. I felt a thing and I did the thing I felt. Because there would always be another Peter. There would always be another man willing to take me out to dinner, and talk about life, and then fuck me. And while I enjoyed the attention, I didn't *need* it anymore. I didn't need sexual attention (that inevitably left me disappointed). I didn't have to try it out with every guy I found attractive. I could just do what I want. I could just do what I want. I could just *not* do anyone I wanted to *not* do.

That's the thing about liberation—it sets you free. I didn't owe Peter (or any man) an explanation. I didn't owe men any level of sex simply because I was sex positive. I didn't owe men sexual satisfaction just because we'd had a nice time, and I was horny. I didn't owe men shit. The perfect no doesn't need an explanation—it simply comes from my mouth.

A TAD ABRUPT

"You look great," he said.
"I know," I said, but I didn't.

Tad was sitting when the hostess ushered me over to the table. He was drinking a beer. I ordered a diet coke, and quickly told him I didn't drink. I didn't want him to feel slighted, like I wasn't drinking because he made me uncomfortable rather than that I was an alcoholic who hadn't had a drink in over a decade. Having to explain it was never not uncomfortable.

He was dressed like a golfer, or a businessman, or a man from the east coast. He was dressed like a frat boy or my dad forty years ago. His shirt looked like money. I wondered if he was one of those coastal elites' people are always talking about. He looked like the kind of person who would have a keychain from an ivy league. I was more nervous than ever for this first date.

Sitting across the table from me, Tad looked like the pictures on his dating profile. I was deeply worried that I didn't look like mine. I've spent my whole dating life making sure men knew exactly what I looked like. Men worry a woman will show up fatter in person, and women worry that a man will murder them. I was always worried a man would murder me for being fatter in person, so I went out of my way to convey every inch of my size. On this date, though, I wasn't worried about my size so much as my almost-naked face.

I'm wearing makeup in all my dating profile pictures. It's not professional makeup, and it's not even anything super glamorous (a smokey eye is the best I've ever been able to master). But tonight, sitting across the table from Tad, was the first time I'd ever been on a date in my life where I wasn't wearing makeup. I've had boyfriends before, and I'm a pretty low maintenance girl who doesn't wear makeup except on special occasions, but no makeup on a first date? My god, I would never. Until that night, of course, and not exactly by my own choice.

The first time I noticed something wrong with my eye, I just thought it was allergies. If it was allergies, was I allergic to my eye makeup or just life in general—who could say? It wasn't a big deal at first—I could just blink the excess tears away and get back to living life. Then, when it started happening more after I'd moved to Montreal with its cold and windy winters, I thought maybe it was a temperature thing. I tried to ignore it. However, as it progressively got worse (by becoming more frequent and more severe), with the tears welling in my eye and threatening to spill down my face, I just started to leave parties early and accept fewer date invitations. I even left a hot make-out session with an adorable guy because my watery eye was watering, and at the time I found it embarrassing. What would I tell him was wrong with me? Looking back now, it seems truly ridiculous to be embarrassed by something so minor but picture yourself on a date with tears streaming down your face, smearing your mascara, while you're making out with a man 12 years your junior. Leaving without explanation was obviously the best option. A real eye-rish goodb-eye, if you will.

When I'd finally had enough of the nuisance, I went to see an optometrist who sent me to an ophthalmologist who numbed my eye with some drops and THEN STUCK A NEEDLE IN MY TEAR DUCT! That's how they test your tear duct, by the way. HUGE needle, right into that nearly microscopic hole at the inner edge of your eye and then they squeeze out saline. If it backs up and squirts on your face, you got a real problem. If it moves through down into your throat (imagine the feeling of drowning) then you're fine, babe. Sadly, I was not fine. The ophthalmologist sent me to an ocular surgeon and that's where I found out that my tear duct was scarred nearly shut. The only fix was surgery where they basically cut you a new tear duct (something I'd end up needing for my other eye as well a few months later). Thank God for Canadian healthcare amirite?!?

When I asked the surgeon why this was happening to me, the doctor said it was likely genetics. He also said that it was more common in women than men (smaller bone structure or something), but that they weren't quite sure why.

"Is it because of all the crying?" I asked. The doctor didn't laugh (which is probably for the best) though I thought it was hilarious. Joke-bombing aside, I was ecstatic. After years of not knowing and thinking maybe this dripping eye thing would just be my life now, I finally had answers and a solution. I spent the next 3 months dabbing at my eye as tears sporadically trickled down my face and I stopped wearing makeup entirely. I wasn't really a makeup wearer to begin with. I only ever wore it for dates and special occasions. But now that I wasn't able to wear it at all, what would that mean for my dating life?

The night of my date with Tad, I was possibly the most nervous I've ever been on a date (where I wasn't just worried the guy would be weird and embarrass me). I was waiting for my surgery date in a few weeks and because I never knew when my tear duct would act up and tears would start streaming down my face, I was currently avoiding wearing makeup. Well, mostly. I vaguely recall wearing a little bit of powder foundation, which was the most naked my face had been on a date, ever. It's not like I did nothing to prepare for the date—I did my hair nice and curly, and I showed up for the date with a story and explanation about how I couldn't wear makeup anymore. I was armed to the teeth with my logical, coping self-protection. Only, it turned out I didn't need it. I explained my dilemma to Tad who just looked at me and said, "You look great."

"I know," I joked.

"You look beautiful," he reiterated.

I posed with my hands under my chin as coquettishly as I could muster, turning my face down towards my shoulder, blushing. Fat or not, I had always thought myself beautiful with makeup, but finding myself beautiful without it was a whole new level of self-love and appreciation I hadn't yet acquired, dare I say, until that night.

Tad ordered us another round of drinks and I excused myself to go to the bathroom. I don't know if it was the lighting, Tad's validation, or just the feeling of freedom that comes from being appreciated exactly as you are—but my god, I'd never looked more beautiful. Tad had said it, and looking at myself in the bathroom mirror, I saw what he saw.

Tad was from New York and staying at the dingey motel in my small town, which he explained was because the other hotel (the good one) was booked solid. I'd never stayed in the motel and only ever heard about it because this girl I knew in high school once stayed there with her older boyfriend who had been kicked out of his house. Tad and I matched on Tinder. He was only in town for one night, the final night of a business trip for something I wasn't paying attention about. Things were going so well I was already planning a visit to New York in my head. Not for anything serious, just because it'd be nice to travel and be able to fuck someone local.

Tad was like if a button up shirt had done their taxes a month early. He told me about backyard parties in NYC, stories about playing silly games and having a real swell time. He was charming and sweet displaying a level of friendliness I'd always hoped for on dates but rarely got to enjoy. His light brown hair was screaming for someone to mess it up. When we stood up from the table, we were the same height, if even that. I couldn't have cared less. I was definitely into Tad and only noticed because he had been sitting when I came in and I guess we'd just never discussed height.

We left the restaurant together, and I drove us to the weird little motel, which wasn't the worst but was nowhere near the best. Tad kissed me while standing near the kitchenette. I excused myself to go to the bathroom and catch my breath. I excused myself to change my panties.

Panties are one of the only things that really differs as a fat woman. All women fear violence and misogyny. All women fear mockery (though what's being mocked might be different). All women fear abandonment, disappointment, creepiness, boredom. Women fear the worst thing that could ever happen to you and the gentlest of slights as the same. We wouldn't be able to go on dates otherwise. If there wasn't a place in our guts where we pretended that possibly getting murdered was an equal fear to finding out he plays with puppets, we'd never leave the house. I wear granny panties on dates because they're comfortable and absorb sweat where I need them to (between my apron belly and my thighs), and then just before sex, in bathrooms that range from shitty motels to swanky apartments, I sub out my standard panties (now damp with sweat) for a far sexier pristine version.

My go-to pair has red lace that frames my butt-cheeks which are considered both flat and fantastic depending on the angle and who you're asking. I'm so tired of asking anyone who doesn't appreciate them instantly, exactly as they are. I'm too old to feel bad about my body. Except my sweat. I haven't let go of the shame of sweat yet. Sweat is a flashing red light of my fatness. Not every crutch can be given up at the same time. Men have lost the power to hurt me but sweat still has a grip on my heart. One day, I think, I won't change my panties before I let him fuck me. Not today though, not with Tad from New York.

When I come out of the bathroom, Tad kisses me again. Tad removes his khakis and his mask at the same time. He wants to shove his dick down my throat and call me a whore. The change is so abrupt, I almost laugh. Tad is half my size, so there is no danger in his declaration. Part of me doesn't care how he sees me, but one thing I know for damn sure is that I'm not about to let this man call me a whore and not get to cum. I tell him I'm game, because for once I'm up for the bullshit of a man. But, I say, I have to go back to my place and get my vibrator.

"How far away do you live?" he asks neither bothered nor excited, and I am instantly bothered by his lack of excitement.

"Fifteen minutes," I say, "round trip."

He hesitates, "I have to get up early tomorrow," which gets my back up even further. Had he simply been excited or enthusiastic, I would've dashed off home to get my vibrator alone, but his hesitation prickles along my skin. Men love to think themselves sex-positive when how they really behave is sex-selfish. They're only positive in ways that benefit them. They like a woman with a full bush because they like a full bush not because they think a woman has a right to do whatever the fuck she wants with her body. They want you to have the freedom to act like a whore, when you're doing it with them, when it benefits their desires. Men having casual sex are rarely thinking about what might benefit your desires. Men having casual sex are rarely asking what the details of your fantasy are. Women should not have to wait for a relationship to cum.

I wasn't ready to throw Tad in the trash just yet though, so I made him come with me to get the vibrator. He didn't want to, but I stood firm and strong and said that if he didn't come with me, I just wouldn't come back. I was bothered that we even had to have this dialogue, but God did it feel so fucking good and hot and powerful to be standing up for myself. No longer would I take what was offered if it didn't suit my needs. Plus, in all honesty, I wanted to fuck Tad. I wanted to fuck Tad and come and have this great fun memory of our time together. So we drove to my house, and I got my vibrator, and we drove back to the weird little motel in my hometown where Tad and I fucked with a vibrator on my clit until we both came.

I fucked a man who called me a bitch (once) while fucking. We immediately stopped because I told him absolutely-the-fuck-not. I said he could say things like good girl, or little slut, or even call me his favorite whore. All the words that are generally used to bring women down have to be preceded by a kindness. I said the words have to be preceded by a safety that allows me to enjoy them because otherwise I'm just allowing a man to say mean shit to me, and babe that's just not my kink (no kink-shaming though). Bitch was always unacceptable though. He asked why and I told him that bitch was too real. Bitch was still something men who hate women actually call them. Men call me a bitch all the time, particularly in online dating message and the world wide web. Bitch feels scary to me. Bitch reminds me of the hatred of men. A man who calls me a bitch wouldn't struggle to say fat bitch, wouldn't have far to go before he'd be comfortable harming me. Perhaps ironically, I say bitch all the time. Bitch please, bitch what, bitch you can't be serious, bitch bye. There's safety when I say it.

Sometimes I wonder if men have ever thought about the fantasies of women, have ever considered how or why they exist. I wonder how many men hear a woman say she wants to be choked and don't understand that what makes it hot (for some) is the safety in it. We're all just so fucking tired of being on guard in every moment of our lives that it's nice to be able to let go, to release the control to someone else. Without safety, it's just violence. Without trust, it's just an action. The heat comes from the dynamic, the pressure being controlled and released.

I doubt Tad understood any of that, but for all intents and purposes, it didn't much matter. Our size difference and my mental capacity for fantasy would do all the heavy lifting that Tad couldn't (or didn't want to). Tad was a country club guy from New York I'd never see again, I could fill in all the blanks he never thought to.

Tad and I used each other perfectly or enjoyed each other perfectly—perspective is what you make of it. I drove home that night fulfilled and in need of fresh batteries. Tad went back to New York the next day, his Tinder mileage changing from single digits to over 3000km away. A few weeks later, I refreshed my *sync your contacts* on Instagram, and it showed me Tad. It showed me Tad and his girlfriend, which was both surprising and unsurprising at the same time. Tad's girlfriend was thin (aren't they always?). I only point this out because as a fat woman, I know that men have treated me terribly. But then arguably, Tad was treating her terribly. A thin woman was being treated terribly by a man. I couldn't stop thinking about how maybe the problem wasn't being fat but being attracted to men. Men were always treating everyone badly.

Fatness was just the weapon a man might use to beat you down, but when you're laying on the ground beaten, it hardly seems to matter what brought you to your knees. The point is the hurt. The point is the violence. The point is knocking us to the ground. Tad's girlfriend (possibly fiancé) looked very New York, very country club pastels and lace summer dresses. I wondered if he liked to call her a whore. I wondered about their sex.

I wondered if it mirrored ours or if I had been Tad's fantasy—a fat girl to dominate (or just a girl to dominate?). I couldn't help but think of all the people in couples with disappointing truths. Tad was most certainly a dick, cheating on his girlfriend while on a business trip (so fucking cliché).

For weeks after finding out, I wondered if I should tell her. It wasn't loyalty to Tad that kept me silent. I couldn't bring myself to tell her—men aren't the only people that are cruel to fat women, and I've learned from a long history that women very rarely hold the men they care about accountable. Their life was none of my business. Tad's girlfriend would have to look out for herself.

ELECTION NIGHT 2016

In 2016, the company that manages Air Miles had a little baby meltdown and told everyone that their points would be expiring. My generous Aunt, made frantic by the news, gifted her miles to me to use. I did the obvious thing and planned a solo road trip throughout Tennessee and Kentucky. Did I know anyone in those states? Nope. Did I have nostalgic memories or even a real comprehensive reason to go there? Honestly, no. Did I pick Tennessee and Kentucky simply because I'd been watching a lot of Justified as of late? I think we're getting warmer.

    I've always had a real lust for certain types of Americana (mainly those based on food, style, and fun accents while ignoring systemic racism and economic disparity). Perhaps even more important, he further south (and then additionally further east) you go in the United States, the more likely you are to find men who like fat women, which as a fat woman was my favorite kind of men.

    Before the trip, I'd done what any sane single adult would do and bought the tinder upgrade so I could move my location around. I swiped my way through

Appalachia like I was preparing for some kind of music tour (by which I mean sex, which is pretty rock and roll of me if I do say so myself).

My profile read: *Looking for some fun dates and maybe some hot dick* (Ok, so I didn't literally type out HOT DICK, but I mean, the hot dick was implied). And then I included all the dates I'd be in each town (to make it easier to get murdered) to make sure I had as many dates lined up as possible.

Nashville Nov. 7-9
Memphis Nov. 10-13
Paducah Nov. 14
Louisville Nov. 15-17
Corbin Nov. 18
Knoxville Nov. 19-21
Nashville Nov. 22-23

When I tell you what a scheduling nightmare it all became, you have to believe me because *oooh boy* things went sideways whenever given the chance. More on that later. For now, the possibilities were endless. Looking back now, with the clarity of hindsight, I had started swiping way WAY too late. I should've been preparing for this trip for weeks, months even (and also, I should've been way more of a selfish asshole when it came to my own time).

The thing is, I've always been incredibly considerate (I know right, I'm such a saint) of other people's time (which is probably why conversely, I'm super intense when they've wasted mine). All of this is to say that double booking dates was not something that came naturally to me. But, and no real spoilers here, if this trip taught me anything it's that you should ABSOLUTELY double—dare I even say triple—book yourself when on vacation because vacation time is limited, and men can be real flakey pieces of shit (when they're not actively talking you out of going out with them by being incredibly lame/stupid/offensive/boring/etc.). I'm getting ahead of myself though because that's really more of an "entire vacation" problem and we're talking about Nashville right now. Nashville was good to me, mostly.

My first night in Nashville is brutal. I develop a migraine on the second leg of my journey which persists well after checking in and taking a shower. Pain aside, I'm unfazed, because I'd planned the first night as a loss anyway. Even without the migraine I knew I'd need time to adjust. The second night in Nashville is election night 2016.

I let my date pick the bar figuring he'd know somewhere it was safe and fun to go. At this point I was basically preparing for Hilary's presidency, and I wasn't sure we wanted to be an interracial couple on a first date in Tennessee the night the racists lost. The hindsight of this is so painful I want to scream. I still can't believe he who must not be named, those three clowns in a trench coat, that cheese powdered face in a straw wig became the president of the United States (the stain of that shame will remain forever).

The date started out wonderfully. With a diet coke in my hand and a beer in his, we watched the election results roll in like a leaking air mattress you're trying to sleep on. It really hadn't ever occurred to me that Trump could actually win. My naivety and optimistic belief in people clearly know no bounds. I mean, he's not even a charismatic asshole, he's just a real gross and pathetic monster propped up by other rich white men and disgusting values.

Yet here we were, two hours into what would have otherwise been a not-bad first date, and both our hearts were being slowly broken in real time. I would put more attention on how terrible this must've been for my date to watch except that I don't really know. First dates are usually full of talking about jobs and friends and ways you like to have fun and not so much how your country, full of racist white people, has continued and will continue to let you down as a Black man in America. Still though, I think it's safe to guess because even as a privileged white Canadian woman, I was devastated (and it wasn't even my country). Nonetheless, the conversation somehow managed to be good and fun and flirty but honestly, there just came a point when we had to call it a night. Looking back now, it's so wild I didn't fuck my date—I mean, I already had a hotel room and no plans for the evening. But, when I tell you that watching a country flash before your eyes is a bit of a boner killer, you can understand my hesitancy.

When I had left the hotel on my way to the bar to meet my date, I hadn't planned to fuck him because I was nervous and scared and in a strange place. Outside the bar, my date walked me to my rental car, which was pretty cute and gentlemanly. We both stopped short of the car to discuss maybe seeing each other again while I was still in town. At that point, I didn't plan to fuck him because I thought we would hang out again (and that time we would fuck). He was going to text on my last night if he was arrived back in town in town (something about having to drive to bowling green for a work thing tomorrow). And then he leaned in and kissed me.

Making out on the side of the road in Nashville on my first night out in town seemed like a pretty good start to my trip. It started to rain while we were kissing and damn if we weren't just a couple of cuties in our own romcom (minus the devastation of the election results). We parted lips and then parted ways. Seconds later, I mixed up the unlock/alarm button on the unfamiliar key fob and promptly set off the piercing alarm of my rental car. *Smooth as silk baybee!*

We ended up texting but never hanging out again. He didn't get back into town in time to hang out, and truthfully, I wasn't that bothered. We weren't soulmates, just two people having fun and trying to make their schedules fit. But after the devastation of the election, in some ways it was hard to regroup—at least with the same person.

On the way back to my hotel that night I stopped to get food at waffle house which isn't as good as an orgasm but *like, wasn't nothing, ya know?* I ended up eating my less than satisfactory meal in my hotel room (which tbh sounds like the level of sexual satisfaction a cishet woman usually gets from a random hookup). Nobody told me that you're only supposed to eat breakfast foods at Waffle House. Yet another lesson I was learning as a grown up.

A NASHVILLE TWIN

My third night in Nashville, I went on a second first date (omg am I a math genius?) with another guy from Tinder. His name was Brendan or Brandon or Braden or something like that. Growing up in the eighties, we were always given the trope of someone who can't remember the names of people they fucked as being some kind of a lothario or player, but the truth is it's far more about how old you are, how much sex you have, and how many mothers named their fucking sons Andy in a single generation, amirite (try a little creativity eh? Marilyn). But I digress, what I really mean to say is that my ability to remember a man's name is directly related to how boring the experience was. Good or bad, if nothing elaborate or transformative happens or if I don't get to cum, then a dude can fuck right off because he'll never get more than a nickname based on some obscure detail I can remember, if even that.

So back to, uh I don't know, "Nashville Guy #2" (sorry bro). I remember that he was attractive enough, he was available, and he was proactive. By which I mean that he suggested a time and a place; he made a plan, and that was enough for me. While I could sit here and talk about how low of a bar that seemed to be (a man who can ask to see you and then set a time and a place), I was on vacation so that meant I was pretty much up for anything, even if I had to limbo to get there.

We met at a bar in downtown Nashville. He drank beers and I drank diet cokes and we talked and laughed and laughed and laughed. Was he particularly witty? Probably not, but he asked lots of questions and I asked lots of questions and we both told stories and made jokes, and we were both in good moods, and we were adults sexually attracted to each other. People will tell you all these terrible things about first dates, but honestly— unless you're a total dud—it's kind of hard to fuck up a first date, especially when at least one of you is on vacation. Because let's be honest, vacation Vicki? That bitch is a good time. She's practically laughing before you've even told the joke. I'm not saying that every first date is going to lead to the connection of a lifetime, far from it. But every adult *should* be able to make conversation for a few hours with someone new without it being a nightmare. The obvious caveat to this is when someone has lied with their pics or about their height or some other major detail that makes them seem sketch. Luckily, neither of us had done any of those things. Not to mention, there's something to be said for *leaning in* and just having a good time because you want to. That's what we were doing. Or maybe he found me majestic. I mean, obviously that's a real possibility, but it's neither here nor there.

The important part is that I was intrigued by him. I liked his southern accent. I liked how assertive he was (I had forgotten how much I deeply enjoyed that about Americans and confident men everywhere). I liked the way he said, "You're good," the same way I say, "No worries."

While we were sitting at the bar, one of the musicians of the band walked around with a hat for tips. When he approached us from behind (out of my view), I had been so rapt by our conversation that he startled me, and I screamed (like a totally normal person). I swear the bar went silent but that's probably just a case of dramatic misremembering. At some point, we went to another bar for another set of beers and diet cokes, and before long he was asking if I wanted to come back to his place. I did.

I didn't invite him back to my hotel because there was only a bed and a chair in my room, and in 2016 I was still doing things to make sure dates didn't go too fast. In 2016, I would still purposely not shave my legs for a first date so that I'd have another reason to offer up other than, "I don't fucking want to, yet," in response to the question, "should we fuck?". In 2016, I was still putting up barricades to protect myself against the sweeping tide of male-boundary-crossing. But that night in Nashville, I *had* shaved my legs. I was ready to fuck.

So, when he said, "Do you want to come back to my place?" even though I had a perfectly good hotel room with a king-sized bed, and smooth as silk legs, I said, "Sure."

Because I wanted to sit on a couch before we fucked. I wanted the sexual tension that builds in the time it takes to watch a movie, I wanted to talk and laugh more and then I wanted to feel that feeling when you know you both want to kiss and fuck but someone has to make the first move. I like the feeling of waiting for the first kiss. I like watching a man while he decides when and how to make the first move. I like watching him struggle, just a little, as a treat.

Outside the bar, we went to our respective cars, and I followed him back to his place.

Now, I want to be clear that I'm not really suggesting that this is safe behavior (nor am I suggesting that it's not), but I was making a calculated decision about my safety, and it was the right decision for me. That said, during the 30-minute drive to his place during which he absolutely seemed to take a wrong turn or two, did I consider pulling a quick turn and dashing back to my hotel no fewer than six times? You're goddamn right I did—especially when he seemed to get confused by a straight-forward detour. Was I about to get murdered? Probably not, but it did cross my mind once or twice.

And then suddenly we were there sitting on his couch making out. It wasn't long before he told me that his roommate was in the other room (which was a real fucking shock given that we'd been making out in the living room for at least twenty minutes, and I hadn't a clue there was anyone else in the apartment). I immediately wished we'd gone back to my hotel instead. We went to his room for a little privacy and dear reader, that's when things got dodgy. Well, maybe not dodgy but definitely sadder.

The man had a twin bed.

The man had a twin bed! I repeat this fact because I need it to sink in. I, a fat woman (a fat woman of age no less), had stumbled into a hookup with a man (a grown goddamn man), with a twin-size bed in his bedroom.

And you're absolutely right, I should've left immediately. No fat woman has ever had good sex on a twin bed and this night would be no different. I remember thinking how misguided I was about what kind of lover he'd be. During our conversation, he'd seemed so intelligent, thoughtful, aware. But the sex was mostly just a mess of sheets and a lot of rapid thrusting (that I tried not to laugh at). Come to think of it, this was all starting to remind me of the detour he struggled to navigate on our drive over here. The man couldn't follow a detour nor find a clit, it would seem. And before you ask if I came—of—course—I—fucking—didn't! Bitch, I was just trying to keep myself on the bed most of the night.

He didn't go down on me, and I didn't ask him to (and I definitely didn't go down on him). To be honest, once all the frantic thrusting began, my desire was dead and I mostly just wanted to get out of there, which I did quickly (the same way he finished lol). Luckily, I managed not to run into his roommate as I scurried my way out the door, literally holding my laughter in with my hand over my own mouth.

Was it the hot sex I had hoped for? Absolutely not. Was it worth going out on a first date in Nashville for? Also no. But the overall experience had been worth it. Though it would be years before I understood that he one hundred percent should not have gotten to cum if I wasn't also cumming, I'd had a fun night, and though his name would fall through my sieve of a memory before I even returned home from my trip, the experience of this adult man genuinely trying to fuck on a twin-size bed will live on in my memory forever. And for that I practice gratitude.

MISGIVINGS IN MEMPHIS

Memphis is when my heart breaks. Memphis is a perfect storm of fear and hurt, bad judgments and misunderstandings. Everything in Memphis is heightened because I'm alone and I think I'm brave which looks like a constant battle between what would be comfortable (staying home and never having any adventures) and what could be considered reckless (something I no longer have faith I can discern one way or the other). In Memphis, I become untethered.

Travelling alone is a tricky thing. It gives off this impression that you're fearless, but the truth is you're terrified and just doing it anyway (which is what having courage is, I have been informed by my therapist). I regularly forget this fact on solo trips. I gaslight myself into thinking I have to enjoy every moment because I was the one who chose to take this trip and so if I'm not having fun, it's somehow my fault for choosing to go. I still haven't figured out exactly why I'm like this—why I put so much pressure on myself to have a good time. It's probably a mix of perfectionism, people pleasing, and the (erroneous belief) that I'm in control of a lot more than I am. Finally, it might have to do with heightened awareness of sadness. Having spent so much of my life suffocated by depression, I have both a heightened awareness and distrust of sadness. I'm always on guard watching out for a depressive episode, always looking for a silver lining or an emotional safety rope to keep myself tethered to happiness. So, when things go awry, they can never just be "awry," I've got to make sure it doesn't escalate to something more intense, prolonged, all-consuming—a depressive episode.

I haven't had a depressive episode since February. The summer after grad school, I went off my anti-depressants (looking back now that seems insane but at the time, I was doing great, and it seemed like all my big stressors were gone). That's yet another stupid thing about depression (and probably mental illness in general)—you spend your life oscillating back and forth between the belief that it's situational and the belief that it's genetic. So, when the stress of grad school was over, it seemed totally logically to go off my meds. And for a while, it was. That's the way it is though. Depression lurks in corners not under spotlights.

The older I get, the more it seems that my depression starts situationally (even it continues long after that thing matters to me). Something in my life going terribly wrong can start a depressive episode. Actually, that's not numerically accurate. Usually, one bad thing doesn't faze me. One frustration or one disappointment is nothing. I'm surprisingly a pretty positive—make the best of things—kind of person. It's when the bad things pile up, one upon the another, that the depression sneaks in. I'm guessing. I always say I'm guessing because it's not exactly feasible to conduct an experiment with my own mental health. Was it the third shitty thing that pushed me over the edge or was it just bad timing? Does a third bad thing simply happen the same day an episode takes hold and because of the episode, the third bad thing feels heavier when I might have otherwise glided past it? I might never know.

    A perfect example of this is two years ago (back around the time of Oleg and Hakeem and somewhere in the middle of the three Andys). A depressive episode begins on Valentine's Day (coincidentally or for all the obvious reasons, I'm not entirely sure). I was house-sitting and waiting to hear back from a publisher about my first book.

    When the rejection from Oleg appeared as a lack of interest in removing obstacles, the hurt was manageable. I could still feel the joy of our time together. When the rejection from Andy #2 (the Juan that I wanted) gave me a laugh if not orgasmic satisfaction, I was jilted but not broken. I checked my phone for messages from Hakeem and saw nothing. Perhaps, he is waiting for the pressure of Valentine's Day to pass, I think. But, when the twenty-one-year-old who has been texting me for four months, and has semi-flaked twice, texts to say that he's working late and can't make it tonight, the wires holding me together snap and I blow away like a loosed parade balloon—ready to destroy everything. I start to google the height of bridges, the speed of trains; I am suddenly a mathematician doing calculations far exceeding my abilities. In the car with the music too loud, I scream and hope to rupture my vocal cords (maybe if I never had to speak again things would be better). What was calm and stable only minutes ago has become a deluge of rage and sadness; the bank of sanity breaks free. I am back to being a horrible person. I won't see it till I'm on the other side, but this is depression. This is an episode.

I'm not depressed when I arrive in Memphis. In fact, I'm not even sad. I had two fun though admittedly bizarre and orgasm free encounters in Nashville, and though Trump had won the election, I was still optimistic about my trip. Arriving in Memphis, I was ready to take advantage of all the work I'd put in on Tinder getting ready for this. I had been swiping my ass off in order to line up some connections. I had planned to stay four nights in Memphis which, not to be greedy, meant the possibility of four dates. Before I'd even left for the trip, I'd lined up two dates—Stephen for Friday (my second night) and Phil for Saturday (my third). That left the night of my arrival and the night before my departure open for possibilities.

Pulling into the hotel thruway on Thursday night, I was full of optimism and potential. As soon as I entered my hotel room, I got to work swiping on Tinder and giving out my snapchat to anyone who seemed promising. Within an hour I had a date and began the process of getting ready. I can't even stress how many hours of my life have been spent (wasted) getting ready (and how much I want them all back). All the hours spent doing my hair and makeup, bent over with a hot hair dryer scrunching and bunching my curly hair while trying not to sweat faster than the hairdryer could dry, wearing uncomfortable bras and suffering through jewelry I was allergic to (read: basically, anything within my budget). All for what? To look only slightly better for some mediocre man with an even more mediocre dick? God, I was an idiot (but we all have our own journey to take, and I was still pretty early on mine).

The worst part about all the effort it takes to get ready is that I was doing it for a man I'd only just matched with and who, unbeknownst to me at the time, was about to absolutely blow it (while simultaneously destroying what remained of my faith in humanity). When I was ready, I messaged and asked where he wanted to meet. Instead of the expected answer, he wanted to know if we'd be fucking later that evening should he deign to waste a couple hours taking me out for a drink.

You're probably thinking, *well that's not how he put it though, right?* And you're right in that he didn't say exactly that, but it was different by a margin of almost nothing. Obviously, I wasn't about to give a man I'd never met, in a city I'd never been to before, a fucking guarantee, literally. Frustrated and fuming, I told him that we should just call it off and was met with *fat bitch* this and *dumb slut* that before I was able to block him. I took off my makeup and jewelry, crawled into bed, and cried myself to sleep still hopeful that tomorrow would be better.

Because I was on vacation, in a city of men I had assumed would love me (or at least be interested enough to want to spend an hour or two together before fucking), my expectations (and the pressure I felt to meet them) were like a foot on the back of my neck. I wouldn't claim that I've ever dealt with disappointment with an *oh well, no biggie* attitude, but there was something about being alone on this trip that made this one man who saw me as nothing more than a warm body to masturbate truly devastating.

The craziest part of the whole scenario is that I probably would've fucked. If we had gone out for a drink, and he had just been a normal human person who was capable of functioning in a social situation, I probably would've fucked him. I was ready to fuck someone. I was on vacation, and I just wanted to have fun and get fucked and that's how easy it is. It is so easy, my gawd. And yet man after man talks himself out of getting laid because he's too stupid and, ya know, a misogynist. It is unbelievably easy to get laid as a man, and frankly, men who aren't getting laid should really look at themselves more honestly. The silver lining of the whole dehumanizing situation was that I was in a hotel, which meant that there were several (honestly too fucking many) pillows on the bed, so when I had dampened one to an uncomfortable degree with all my tears, I simply switched it out for another to fall asleep on. Am I not the luckiest girl in the world, or what?

The thing about the problems happening in Memphis was that they were mostly philosophical. When my iPhone malfunctioned prior to my trip, I wasn't that bothered. I went to the Apple store, got the issue fixed and carried on. When the engine light came on in the rental car, I didn't freak out. I googled the symbol only to realize it was just the tire pressure light, promptly filled up those rubber babies and kept driving. Not a tear was shed. Not a meltdown was had. But dealing with misogynistic men who only viewed me as free pussy when I had expected to be having so much fun on so many different dates? There wasn't an easy fix for that except to maybe stop having expectations—to which I would say, I dare you to try! Or, to stop dating men entirely—to which I would say, I'm honestly considering it.

The next morning, I woke up to a text from Stephen. Stephen was memorable from the moment we matched. I don't usually put that much weight on a person's appearance (because being attractive has zero correlation to whether or not I'll get to orgasm), but Stephen was off-the-charts hot. Stephen was model hot, like famous person without being famous hot. His profile said he was 6'4 (as confirmed by his university basketball stats after a quick google). Stephen was jacked, and his face was gorgeous (not to mention his hair was lined up perfectly in every single photo). Swiping through his Tinder profile, it was nothing but stylish business suits (obviously tailored to highlight his muscles), golfing pics with his dad (aww), and the occasional gym flex. It was also clear that he was a professional with money (which made sense later when I found out he was in the banking industry). There wasn't a fish in sight except for the feeling I had that he had (had to!) to be a catfish. But like I said, I had already googled him and so I knew the man was real. Still though, still, I couldn't help but wonder if the man in the pictures while admittedly real and living in Memphis, could be someone other than the person I was texting. I waited for the other shoe to drop.

    Stephen texted Friday morning to cancel our date that because he was coming down with a cold. Stephen could've said he was cancelling because he was having emergency foot amputation surgery, and I would've found it more believable. You have to remember that we were living in a pre-pandemic world, and I couldn't understand why someone would bail on a once-in-a-lifetime chance to meet me. He told me that he was going to go for a steam later and if he felt better, he'd let me know. It felt like a brush off. It felt personal. It felt like bullshit. I couldn't deny that him cancelling was both incredibly disappointing because I'd given him the coveted (or not, as evidenced by him cancelling) position of the Friday night date. Did he think there would be another chance to meet? I was disappointed and livid. Memphis was really starting to suck.

I'm not poor, in the sense that my family is middle class and we're rich adjacent (hence all the holidays and vacations, like this one, that I've gotten to go on because of some gift or sharing of a family member. I myself am broke. I have little to nothing. I have degrees and a lot of student debt. I have no financial assets. My bank account is rarely anything but empty and when it's not, it's usually because someone has gifted me something. I have a MacBook because my relatives bought it as a graduation gift after earning my masters. I've never gone hungry, and I've never not had a roof over my head, but financial stability is not in my past, present or likely future. All of this is to say that I have a complicated relationship with vacations given that I can't really afford them and yet somehow seem to be on a lot of them. More important to my point is the pressure I put on myself to have fun on them. I say myself because it doesn't seem that anyone else has ever put pressure to have fun upon me, so my only explanation is that it's self-imposed. I think I blame myself for being an overly educated artist who lives beyond her means, so I feel the need to justify every expenditure. If I'm not having fun on a vacation than I'm an idiot who made the wrong choice. I must've made a bad decision either in where I've chosen to go or what I've chosen to do.

On Friday, after finding out Stephen has the sniffles, I buy a ticket for Graceland and try to enjoy it, but I'm almost in tears when I realize I've spent $75 USD to see a "mansion" that's not much bigger than my aunt's house. When I eat the BBQ that is not particularly great, I lament how foolish I am to have taken a thin friend's advice on food. When my date cancels, I can't remember why I even wanted to come to Memphis. Everything is clouded by pressure and the emotions that fall from crumbling under it.

Still scarred from the misogyny of my first night in Memphis, I didn't bother swiping for a backup. I still had a date booked for the next night and given my emotional state, I figured self-care was more in order than male validation and thus, I went for BBQ. If I wasn't going to be getting any dick, the least I could do was stuff myself some satisfying meat. Unfortunately, I went to a place my small, thin friend had suggested (clearly an error in judgement I should've known better than to trust). Eating the meal back in my hotel room, I was less than thrilled. The meat was drier than my pussy, which was starting to feel like a theme for Memphis. I tried not to cry about how poorly things seemed to be going. I knew I was being a huge baby, but the sadness was visceral. With my mouth stuffed with brisket, I text Stephen on to see how he's feeling. He confirms that he's sick, and I no longer care. I'm not sure if I replied or not, but if I did, I'm sure it was a passive aggressive: *ok*. I assume he was a catfish. He couldn't bring himself to meet because he wasn't real. I watch law and order in my hotel room and go to sleep, after swapping wet for dry pillows.

I woke up Saturday morning unsurprisingly in a funk. I could've probably dealt with one thing but shitty men, flakey men, AND shitty BBQ in what was seemingly the BBQ capital of the world was a bridge too far for me. I had to do something to turn my trip around (not to mention get me in a better mood for my date with Phil that night). Phil and I had been messaging long enough and with enough frequency that we'd already added each other to facebook. He was a tall, bald, age-appropriate black man and, at least before arriving in

Memphis, I couldn't have been more excited to meet. Both Phil and Stephen had me incredibly excited for my time in Memphis and even though both night one and two had gone to the shitter, I was hopeful for night three. Things with Phil were bound to work out because we had plans. WE HAD PLANS!

Determined to improve my mood and take in some of the sights of Memphis, I buy a ticket to the National Civil Rights Museum and spend two hours walking through history. Every website and good book had suggested the museum, so I figured it was a safe bet.

The museum, like the history of civil rights in America, is devastating. I hold my tears until I'm back at my car (it feels like my white woman tears should not have space in this museum—if anywhere). After the museum, my mood slithers like ooze down a drain. The idea of ever having fun again seems impossible. I know this all seems so dramatic and disproportionate to what is actually happening on my trip but there's something about being alone in a place you've never been before that heightens every emotion (particularly the negative ones). Not to mention that virtually every interaction on Tinder is with a man who doesn't view women as human. Disappointments have piled upon disappointments have sunk into my bones.

Before my trip, and with a misguided impulse, I messaged a friend of mine on facebook to ask for recommendations for food and fun in Memphis since her boyfriend was from there, and they had visited often. She gave a couple suggestions for BBQ (which we've quickly seen were terrible) and then ended the message by saying that I shouldn't go downtown in Memphis on a Saturday night unless I wanted to get stabbed. If I had any sense, I would've seen through the BBQ fiasco to know that her judgement couldn't be trusted and not heeded her warning. Instead, I let it derail me.

Should I have let one disappointing BBQ experience ruin my vacation? Obviously not. But would I? That was yet to be determined. The more pressing question was should I (a woman of strength and girth who can handle herself in pretty much any situation)) have listened to my small, petite friend and her equally as petite boyfriend about where and when a place is safe? No, probably not. People are mostly babies and generally not qualified to give advice. Allow me to explain: Vancouver's downtown eastside is world renown for drugs and homelessness, but as a local I know that it's perfectly fine place to be (at least in terms of safety). I might've been able to think all this through clearly had I been in the right state of mind, but that wasn't the emotional state I was in at the time—that's hindsight for you.

Back at my hotel after the museum and riddled with anxiety, I text Phil. I hesitantly ask about our date tonight. He suggests we shoot pool (which is something I love to do) at a place downtown. The same downtown that I was expressly told by my friend and her boyfriend not to go to on a Saturday night, and this was, in fact, Saturday night. Except it wasn't just my friend who'd freaked me out. The night before, while swiping for matches on Tinder (and literally swiping right on everyone to increase my chances), I'd matched with a cop. I was intrigued because he was a Black police officer (God, I was naïve back then). We briefly chatted on the app, but he was working so there was no chance of meeting. I told him I was going to be going to downtown on Saturday night and he told me to be careful. I had never been such a baby before but here I was now afraid to go out to meet Phil at a place downtown.

I explained this to Phil. I told him about my friend and the cop and how I was just feeling really anxious, and *could we meet somewhere else?* Instead of suggesting another place, he doubled down, saying that it would be fine, and I should just go, and then switched gears and suggested we go out the next night instead. I couldn't understand why that bar was so special to him that we couldn't just meet somewhere else. In fact, on the heels of all the other things I was worried about, Phil now being weird instead of just comforting me really rubbed me the wrong way. I cancelled completely and that was that. Another night in Memphis, another batch of tear-stained pillows.

Were men really the problem with my time in Memphis? Obviously yes. If accuracy is something you pride yourself on though, I should probably add that it was more of a perfect storm of several shitty things coming together (men included, men are always terrible enough to be included) that resulted in my mostly shitty time in Memphis.

It's never the first blow that knocks you to the ground. One disappointment is manageable. Two is a by-product of living a human life. By the time the fifth disappointment clobbers you, your eyes are blurry with tears, and you never saw it coming. That's what Memphis feels like. When Sunday arrives, I've all but given up.

With no dates in hand and nothing to do but enjoy the city and relax, I took myself first to a coffee shop where I tried to write but instead found myself having to choke back tears before eventually leaving (for fear of sobbing in public). The only thing left that I could think of to potentially save my mood was to go for a walk along the river. When they say that exercise releases endorphins, they're not exaggerating because after no less than ten minutes of fresh air and exercise, my mood was turning around. After thirty minutes, I was a new woman. *What the fuck was I doing letting all these men and anxieties get the better of me?!* I was in Memphis for the first (and potentially only) time in my life—I owed it to myself to try and enjoy it. After my revitalizing walk, I drove over to a café and then walked around the neighborhood just people watching, window shopping, and just generally (finally!) enjoying myself. And then Stephen texted.

Stephen asked what I was up to, and I told him. He asked where I was, and I told him. I walked for a few more minutes and then heard someone calling my name. I turned around and there, leaning against his car, was Stephen. Stephen—looking exactly like his pictures, Stephen. Stephen—not a catfish, Stephen. Stephen—didn't think he was real, *Stephen*! I could hardly believe my eyes and was also confused. I had assumed the whole "being sick thing" was a bullshit excuse to get out of meeting up because he was a catfish. But here he was, dressed like an ex-NFL player stretching his golf clothes to the limit of their tailored fit. Had he really cancelled just because he felt like he was coming down with a cold? Was this herculean looking man really that big of a fucking baby?!

Stephen showed up leaning against his BMW looking like a goddamn golf model with no real good explanation for anything. He stuck to his claim that he was sick. I motioned at his outfit and the fact that he'd just been playing golf. "For work," he said, something about clients or whatever. I couldn't hear; my ears were filled with rage like cotton. We talked for a about ten minutes—me telling him about the shittiness that had been Memphis, and him talking about how cute and pretty I was and how sorry he was that I wasn't having a good time. Everything he said sound muffled by my mood. He noticed I was pouting and asked for a hug. "I have to go to this banquet thing tonight," he said apologetically, "otherwise we could make up for everything tonight."

"If you weren't sick," I interjected.

"If I wasn't sick," he smiled.

"Maybe we could meet up after the banquet?" he asked, or maybe I asked, I'm not really sure anymore. But we didn't meet up. He was sick, he wasn't feeling well, he couldn't make it. He said words but none of them made sense. He hugged me again before leaving. I couldn't understand the point of any of this. He said I was beautiful, my body banging. He said how glad he was that we had at least gotten to meet, if only for a moment.

"Yeah," I rolled my eyes, "only for a moment." I turned to walk away after saying goodbye.

"Keep in touch?" he said, and I nodded and waved.

Back at the hotel I realized what had happened. I don't know why I hadn't thought to look for it before, but I did a fresh sync of my contacts and found him on Instagram. Instagram is where all, or at least a few, answers can always be found

On his Instagram, I saw his girlfriend (who btw became his fiancée and I'm fairly certain by the press of this book, his wife). I'll never understand why he wanted to meet me at all—it was like cheating but without any of the good parts. Why not just ghost me if he hadn't wanted to actually meet, to fuck? Why the rouse about being sick? Why the rouse about anything? Just unmatch after the first hit of validation (which is the only thing I can figure you'd be on Tinder for if you didn't actually intend to cheat). Unless he'd wanted to cheat but hadn't found me hot enough to bother (except he'd gone out of his way to meet me, eventually). It just didn't make sense. Plus, I know he found me attractive because he continued to text for years after that chaste first meeting. He wanted me, that much I knew. I just couldn't figure out why he hadn't just *had* me. Maybe the fantasy was all he could handle. But even then, why bother to meet on a Sunday, fully clothed, in broad daylight, on a street in Memphis? It was a bit like going to a chocolate shop just to look at the bars. Then again, I doubt people go home and jack off to chocolate bars. I guess for some men, the fantasy is enough (and a woman's time worth nothing to them).

LOUISVILLE SLUGGER

Hitting the road again after Memphis filled me with relief but not because I expected the men of other cities to be different. It wasn't the men of Memphis that had brought me to my knees (metaphorically only, of course) but misogyny.

It was misogyny all along!

The patriarchy is everywhere (including dating apps). But something happened to me in that town that changed me forever and for the better. I hate the idea that a person has to experience hardship to grow but for all the heartache and frustration Memphis had brought me, it shifted something in me.

In Paducah, after checking into my hotel, I got dressed and went out for a drink. I was still sober, but I refused to believe I couldn't still sit at a bar and order diet cokes and just live. I didn't bother swiping much in Paducah. I would only be there for one night and I was still up to my ears in disappointment from men (even if I'd developed a better perspective on it).

Paducah is small town, so it shouldn't have been surprising when the bartender and another customer started talking about welfare moms. The bartender assured me she knew real live actual women who had babies for no other reason than the government assistance. She lamented how unfair that was given that she was busting her ass as a bartender putting herself through business school. I didn't want to shame her for her (bullshit) views, so I asked her if she thought those women were doing well. Though I admittedly did not believe she knew these women (or had any real understanding of their lives), I continued to question her. Did she think having a child was easier than bartending? How big did she think welfare cheques were? I asked her if she thought motherhood was only a desire that rich people have? I asked her if she thought children deserved to suffer because their parents were idiots? Before long the conversation pivoted to opioids and again, I found myself taking up the cause she was against. How could you not try to help people who were suffering? Did she think people suffering from addictions were doing well, like did she think they were thriving with clear minds and full bank accounts? Did she think they were wholly to blame for a flawed medical system and even further flawed humanity where being a billionaire is fine but the people who flip your burger don't deserve healthcare? I doubt I convinced her of much, except maybe Canadians are preachy saps, but I'll be honest that when the customer to my left started leaning towards our conversation to hear better and one of the line-cooks came out on his break to sit and talk, it's possible a difference was made—even if just of perspective. I tipped her well and left, another brave night of going out alone under my belt. I tucked myself under the covers of my room at the Best Western Paducah and changed my Tinder location to Louisville for the following few days.

In Louisville the next night, I took myself out to a college basketball game, which let me tell you had the stadium and fans of a professional league anywhere else (those people are serious about their sports). The next day I went to Churchill Downs (home of the Kentucky derby) where I placed a few bets and watched some horses run. Later that night I took myself out for a Hot Brown (which is a sandwich *not* a man for anyone confused) at the Brown Hotel Lobby Bar. I even made friends with a woman who turned out to be starting a master's program in Creative Writing the following semester. During our conversation she divulged that she'd recently gotten married. She told me that she wore red shoes with her dress.

"Like, clown shoes?" I asked confused (and accidentally showing my feelings about marriage).

She laughed before showing me a picture of red stilettos to clarify.

The next night, bolstered by my friend making capabilities and Louisville just generally feeling like the soft landing I needed, I accepted a date with guy from Tinder.

And then I cancelled the date with the guy from Tinder. Unlike the misogyny of Memphis, the reason I cancelled was much less upsetting and more the speed of bullshit I was used to back home. Like most men (interested in me) before him, my Tinder date was quick to ask me out and then just as quick to be nonchalant about planning it. He said he was studying, and he'd text me when he was done but I can't stand nonsense like that. Sure, if we're friends, you can have loose plans with me. But a date? A date with a stranger? I'm not waiting around all night twiddling my thumbs without a timeframe or a location. So even though he was polite, and cute, and clearly interested, I cancelled and said it was not going to work. And then I went out to buy some grocery store salads.

I can't remember if I was wearing a shirt with no bra or if I was wearing a bra but no shirt under my sweatshirt. When I ran out to the store, I had planned to make it quick and hadn't dressed for a date. I'd barely dressed to be out in public. In 2016, I still thought men gave a shit about that kind of thing. In 2016, I still thought an ugly bra could ruin a boner. This is why, when my Tinder date-no-longer-date texted to say fuck it we should just meet at a bar right now, I was hesitant. My boobs were either out loosey-goosey or they were contained in a bra that would seem insane should anyone unzip my hoodie. I was wearing jeans (and I wouldn't normally wear jeans on a date because of how they make my stomach look bigger—or exactly as it is which feels bigger when you're insecure about it).

I wanted to say no because I wasn't properly prepared. I wanted to say no because I was nervous. We met at a bar thirty minutes later because I was trying to be the kind of person who would meet a man for a date at a bar either not wearing a bra or just being sloppy with it.

Both the bar and my date were extremely weird in a truly delightful way. He was a big nerd (which is something that rarely gets represented in the media). Black men are rarely given the luxury of being nerds and though I doubt it had been given to him, my date had taken it as his right and goddamn it that was hot af. The bar kind of felt like an auditorium of theatre kids having drinks at band practice and I loved it. There were a few bikers that felt like the supervising teacher who volunteered to be with the kids just so they wouldn't get up to trouble and because they knew that they were good at their core. When my date put his hand gently on my thigh, it was warm and endearing. He only got more complex as we talked.

"What are you studying for?"

"Firefighter entrance exam," he said proudly.

"That's amazing," I beamed both because I love a sexy stereotype and also a hero. "When is the exam?"

"Tomorrow at 7am," he said to my shocked face.

Suddenly I felt terrible for dragging him away from his studying. Or, well, mostly terrible, I mean he was also super-hot and fun, and I was having a great time. Plus, you know, I didn't want to infantilize him (or whatever I had to tell myself so I wouldn't be bummed out on his behalf). He was an adult who could make his own informed decisions, which is the mantra I repeated to myself over and over again as we drove (separately) back to my hotel suite.

Back at my hotel we spent the next few hours having a truly lovely time. I hadn't brought my vibrator on the trip (like an absolute fucking idiot) so going into things, I hadn't expected that I'd get a chance to cum. You can imagine my surprise then when this stranger, this Louisville slugger (sorry! I'm a sucker for a double baseball/sex/location triple entendre), spread my legs apart to bury his face in my pussy. I hate to disappoint you all by informing you that sadly, however much I wanted to, and however good and skilled this man was at finding my clit (which he was, good job sir!), I couldn't get myself over the edge to cum.

Men love to spread this bullshit rumor about how difficult it is to make a woman cum. I call it bullshit because the thing they think is hard is not the thing that is hard at all. Men think it's the physical part that's hard, but if you've ever listened to a woman getting eaten out, she'll tell you exactly what she likes—though it may be her hips or breaths conveying the message. Then there's the rumor that it's harder for a woman to cum, mentally speaking. But I would argue that it's equally easy for men and women to cum (when stimulated correctly) but that it's easier for men to relax in a world designed for them. It's not that women can't get out of our own heads or out of our own way, it's that men have less in their heads and less in their way.

Even in the most literal of ways—my date had less to worry about in terms of being exposed and vulnerable with a stranger in a hotel room. From safety concerns (will he murder me?) to societal issues (what if he doesn't like how my pussy smells or tastes?). And before anyone chimes in with bullshit about how a man might worry about his genital aromas, pretending that there is equal societal pressure for flawless privates is absolute insanity. They don't have a whole line of products at the drugstore for men's ball care and I assure you men's balls are all grosser than any pussy has ever been. But that's the thing about sex and society, women carry the burden.

Now, admittedly, I don't have pussy insecurity (my vagine smells great, tastes great, is great, and if you don't fucking like it that's your goddamn problem and maybe you don't come back to this buffet again). But, for whatever reason, I couldn't relax enough to make it happen. Or, I couldn't relax enough to ask this stranger to use the full force of his face for me to grind my clit on.

Or, I couldn't relax enough because I'd had too many coffees and not enough (read: edibles). Who knows why? The truth is, as much as I am the great crusader of the female orgasm (or at least, I was on my way to being worthy of that crown), I'm not some heartless bitch who thinks a man genuinely trying and being willing to go as long as you need is not without credit. My soon-to-be-fireman did a truly valiant effort and though he never got to feel the gush from my hydrant (okay I may have lost the plot on this analogy but just stay with me), I thoroughly enjoyed our time together. He left the next morning heading straight to his exam (which he passed with flying colors for anyone feeling invested).

The rest of my trip continued in much the same way (with me doing lots of adventurous things solo—like going to Dollywood!) but as the trip inched closer to the end of things, I found myself swiping less and less. Misogyny aside, the frustration stoked by trying to arrange any kind of real date with men on Tinder (while on vacation) no longer seemed worth it. Tennessee and Kentucky had already taught me a lot about disappointment and perseverance and while the lessons were valuable, I wanted to take a breath or two and just relax a bit. Vacation sex, as it turns out, is a bit of a hassle.

When I get back to Vancouver after my trip, I start looking for a job right away. I'm not sure if it's the precarity of my mental health throughout my trip, or all the things that went wrong which harden me, but it's time to step back from writing. I put my unpublished collection of short stories on the shelf. I am determined to grow up and quit fucking around. A friend in Montreal tells me about the company she works at. I send her my resume. I wait with bated breath. The job is to be a copywriter, but when they respond and offer an interview, it's for a job as a scriptwriter at a major adult entertainment brand.

THE LOOPHOLE

Whenever I think about male writers, or more specifically, literature written by male writers, I think about this quote from *The Virgin Suicides* by Jeffrey Eugenides:

> "Her wet hair hung down her back and already her extremities were blue. She didn't say a word, but when they parted her hands they found the laminated picture of the Virgin Mary she held against her budding chest."

It's a scene of suicide but that's not what strikes me. It's the way a woman can't even take her own life without a man focusing on her tits. A woman can't even kill herself outside of the patriarchy. The freedom men must feel every day of their goddam privileged lives. I can barely stand it. I bet male writers don't even notice they're doing it. I wonder if that's why I spend such little real estate in my stories writing about what men look like. I think it comes from a lifetime of standing in a defensive position about my own body. I'm exhausted from being on edge, and also, I think critiquing someone's body is both boring and shitty. Men regularly give me so much material with which to criticize them, it hardly seems worth it to talk about their mediocre bodies. I usually try to be the bigger person, or as Michelle Obama says (totally out of context and not usually something I agree with), "When they go low, we go high." I mention this not because I'm some paragon of ethics but because I'm preparing for you for this final story, in which I absolutely become a hypocrite.

But also, while judging me for my hypocrisy, I beg you to remember that even though I have settled a hundred, nay a thousand times, for a medium-ugly (and that's being generous) man, you don't have to. You don't have to settle for anything less than you deserve. Will that mean you don't get to go on as many dates or let as many losers fuck you in the hopes they value pleasure equality? Yes, probably. But as someone who has run the gauntlet, let me have done it for you—so that you, my precious little angel, don't have to. Or, if you're like me and it's too late, do not let them characterize you as bitter or jaded because you are not. Or, if you are, like me, and the world has shown you no grace and little fun, then you should wear that bitterness with pride.

Bitterness is just another way the patriarchy tries to make women smaller. A woman who is bitter has seen the world of men and lived to tell about it. And baby, they *do not* want you to talk about it, which is yet another reason to be louder. Take up space, use your voice, and when they call you bitter—ask them how they think you got this way. Ask them to explain, to offer proof and evidence, ask them to cite their sources. Teach them with their own ignorance. Or don't. Honestly, it's not your job to educate men (however much they need it).

Months have gone by since our last interaction, years even and then I see him back on Tinder. I swipe right because I want to see if he swiped right on me. I forget everything I know about how often men swipe right on everyone. I start swiping right on everyone because fuck them if men think they can bogart being callous with everyone else's time. I will not allow them to waste my time (I continue to allow them to waste my time). I'm genuinely uninterested in Andy #3 serving anything other than my ego, but memories are fickle systems that have a way of sorting themselves. We match because he's swiped right on me, and I wait to see what he has to say. He messages boring shit and I respond with boring shit and the conversation fizzles. I unmatch.

More months go by, more years even, and there he is again. This time, he gets in a little (through no expertise of his own). That's the thing about men—they have absolutely no idea how often they succeed or fail with a woman based on something that changes with her and has absolutely zero to do with their own words, actions, or appearance. Men will absolutely tell a story about how they bagged a woman and she'll tell the same story to her friends but in her story the main factor is boredom. I can't tell you how many stories I've listened to where men think only they experience boredom, that only they like to fuck for entertainment. And like good for all of us, there's no shame in fucking for entertainment-sake (assuming you're an adult capable of not being a shithead who purposely hurts or deceives anyone).

When Andy #3 and I start chatting again, for what feels like the hundredth time, he's no more interesting or available than any other time. The only change has occurred with me. I'm in the midst of interviewing for a job in Montreal. I'm writing test scripts for adult entertainment. I'm spending my days trying to write raunchy scripts to impress the fuck out of the woman interviewing me. I'm literally sitting at my computer every day, trying to come up with the hottest scenarios and dialogue I can. I'm so turned on that I practically need to put a blanket down on my seat. This is when Andy #3 re-enters the picture—somewhere between unexpected horniness and a hazy memory, Andy slips back in through a loophole. My brain is occupied with trying to get this new job and I forget how wildly irritated (and thus irrational) I became after going out with Andy #3. I forget how little he interested me, how unpleasant I found his voice, how our dates had only gone *so so*. My memory is a traitorous bitch who likes drama, apparently.

His messages pop up while I'm writing scripts. At first, I'm flirting to tease him, to let him dream about what he's missing. I type word after word hoping to earn a spot with [redacted adult entertainment brand] and Andy experiences the best luck of his life—I'm so horny by the time I'm done that I agree to meet up with him. Walking through his front door, I know he absolutely doesn't deserve this, doesn't deserve anything from me (especially not my body). I promise myself that I will not suck his dick and I keep that promise. I show up wearing jeans and a cute shirt under a sweatshirt. I don't bother wearing makeup or curling my hair—I just wear it in a ponytail and then right before knocking on his door I take it down and give it a floof. Tonight, we don't waste time on the couch and go straight to the bedroom. He seems shorter than last time, his arms thinner, his lips more puckered. In his bedroom, we stop kissing and he moves around the foot of the bed to the other side laying open the blankets.

"Get in," he gestures to the bed.

"In our clothes?" I ask, confused (and grossed out).

"Yeah," he nodded, "Is that weird?"

Having been raised right, I answered, "Yes."

I'd never get in a bed, I mean literally between the sheets, with street clothes on. That's gross. Street clothes are dirty. Looking back now, I can't believe I let a man who wears street clothes in his sheets finger me, but we all have regrets and that was only one of many. Instead of making an even bigger thing of it, I simply stripped and climbed in. I mean, we both knew what I had come over for. This wasn't a date; I was there to fuck. Well actually, I was there to fuck and get my pussy ate, emphasis on the pussy eating, something we had already discussed. That's the thing about agreeing to see Andy again. Even though things hadn't gone so well in the past, I had been very clear from the start that things were different this time. I went over to Andy's with the express desire of getting my pussy eaten. He had said he wanted to eat it, and I wanted to get eaten. It seemed a perfect fit.

Andy stripped off his clothes as well and climbed in beside me. We started making out which was normal enough, but it quickly occurred to me that he wasn't good at this. He wasn't good at any of this. He wasn't good at the dating part, and he definitely wasn't going to be good at the fucking part. He didn't know how to touch me, and I don't even mean the intricacies of my pussy. He didn't know how to touch me as a person, as a woman, as a being with tits and thighs and skin. Had this happened when I was younger (even as little as two years ago), I would've assumed it was about me. I would've assumed his trepidation, his timidity, his lack of exploration was all about me and my fatness. Old me would've assumed his lack of ability was a lack of desire, but here in his bedsheets at the age of thirty-five, I knew this almost forty-year-old man was actually just clueless. I couldn't help but think about all the ex-girlfriends he'd had and wondered if they'd been left disappointed by him. Maybe all his ex-girlfriends had been as clueless as him and then I guess it was fine—maybe I just needed to find a sexual match.

While pondering all of this, he shifted from laying on top of me (barely moving, like a real weirdo) to sort of sitting beside me (but like, up by my shoulders) and then he was kind of crouching on his knees but facing towards my feet. I just looked at him confused because honestly, I had no idea what the fuck he was thinking or doing. Maybe he was trying to make a sixty-nine happen? Before I could ask, Andy leaned down and across my torso and tried to lick my pussy. Now, maybe, and I really want to stress this as a maybe because I'm pretty certain I would find this idiotic no matter what my size was, but maybe he'd tried this move on thinner women and it had been successful—but I was a fat woman.

I am a fat woman. I am not coke bottle Marilyn Monroe fat, I'm real fat, super fat. My belly is big and hangs down. Trying to lick my pussy from a position damn near my shoulders may honestly be the dumbest thing a man has ever tried with me. Also worth noting, I have an innie (meaning I have those two fat lips around my clit, all my bits are wrapped up inside) so if you want to suck my clit, you have to spread my lips apart to get in there, and here was this man thinking he could lick my pussy from above and to the right like he was taking his best shot on a goddamn grassy knoll. The stupidity was boundless. But then again, maybe he didn't want to lick it, maybe he didn't want to make me cum, maybe it hadn't even really crossed his mind.

The chronology of sex is a funny thing. It's never this thing where one person is like, "you want to lick my pussy and get me off?" and then other person is like "yes, I will do that now." At least not during casual sex. Or, I mean, maybe there are, and those people would be my communication idols but given what I know about my own sex life and the sex lives of other women, there's usually an ebb and flow to things. Maybe he licks your pussy for a little foreplay and then you fuck and then he finishes you off with more pussy licking to make sure you come. That's probably the standard for hookups (when a woman demands equal pleasure because otherwise it usually just ends after the fucking and you'd better hope that his foreplay licking got you).

Some women love to get off first, but I dry up after I cum and don't enjoy anything in or near my pussy for a bit after, so I don't enjoy cumming first. Plus, I think it's kind of bullshit that if a woman wants to cum, she has to make sure she cums first. If he's not always making you cum regardless of order, he can fuck right off. The thing is though, you rarely know in advance that he's not going to get you off. You rarely know in advance that he'll give you the most pathetic, tepid, and entirely misguided pussy licking of your entire life and then you'll let him fuck because you're still turned on and then he'll cum quickly and pass out beside you. He will actually go right the fuck to sleep never being bothered you didn't cum not for one goddamn second.

You have to remember to be easy on yourself—I tell myself this often while recounting tales of all of the men who've left me unsatisfied. Their shame always feels like my shame because they got to cum. They got to cum. He gets to cum. They all get to cum.

It makes me sick just thinking about the unfairness of it all. Especially because I'm about to tell you that we fucked, and he got to cum. Because after all, I can't see the future. I didn't know that that tepid pathetic little pussy-licking that he'd done, if you can even call it that, it was more like he fluttered his eyelashes at the general direction of my pussy and hoped I'd cum. Obviously, I mean OBVIOUSLY, I didn't cum. But he got to cum. A couple gentle pumps from his longneck-beer-bottle-shaped body and he was done. And I know, I know, we don't body-shame here, but the thing is I'm not better than that, okay well I'm not always better than that because here in the pages of this memoir, in the lines of these short stories, after a man has been an utter and complete fucking disappointment and it's just you and me here talking *girl goss,* I can tell you the truth about his body. I can rip him to fucking shreds. Because he deserves it.

But hear me now, if you are a man who also has a longneck-beer-bottle-shaped body and you bought this book and now you're wondering if your wide hips and cyclist quads are hideous as they sit below your skin on bones upper torso, the answer is no—unless you're a selfish shithead who doesn't value women enough to make sure they experience some pleasure on a night you're shoving your sad little dick in and out of them. If the latter is the case, then yes, get your disgusting stems away from me and maybe start doing some upper body work. But if you're a good guy just feeling insecure about your body, mirrored here in the one I'm critiquing, please know that I don't know a single woman who loves her partner's body, and you actually won the lottery because your body is that of a man which means you get to be anything and it's fine—women will still love you.

But let's get back to Andy and his dipshit antics. It seems too cliché and Andy came and then literally and immediately fell asleep (which, if I'm ever arrested for murder is what you should assume happened prior to me committing said heinous act). I controlled my temper (like a lady) and instead of murdering Andy immediately, I fumed for a few minutes while uncomfortably laying in his bed listening to his breath get louder and louder with every irritating inch he crept closer to REM. I thought about waking him up (by kicking him), but the truth was, I no longer wanted this man between my thighs. Was I furious I had been duped again by another barely decent man who had proven himself even more worthless by not even being able to complete the basic task of a hookup? Absolutely. But did he deserve to be face deep in my pussy after such a pathetic performance? I'd let him starve before letting him take another bite.

I picked up my clothes off the floor and went into the bathroom to change. I didn't want him to get even one more glance of my gorgeous body. By the time I was finished in the bathroom, he had stirred and called out to me.

"You're leaving?" he asked jumping out of bed. I was quickly putting my shoes on.

"Uh...yeah," I responded in an uncharacteristic call to honesty. I've always been honest online, in dating app profiles, in my books, in conversations at parties, but it's rare for me to actually tell a man the ways in which he's disappointed me in real time in his presence. But I'd had enough of this shit and since I'd only given him a second (or one hundredth?) chance because I was all horned up writing porn and agreed to hookup under the basic requirement that it would be pleasurable for me, and he had failed on all accounts, there was nothing to lose by telling him the truth and at the very least I would get satisfaction from telling him what shit lay he was. "You didn't even make me cum."

He looked taken aback like it hadn't even occurred to him that my orgasm mattered (regardless of the fact that we had absolutely discussed it) and then sincerely apologetic, which I found interesting if not satisfying.

"Next time, for sure," he said.

"Unlikely," I said grabbing my umbrella that I'd left leaning against the door.

That night with Andy was like that moment around dusk when it gets so dark you can no longer see but if you just give it one more moment your eyes will adjust, and the moon will do its thing and suddenly you can see everything clearly. Even though it's dark outside. Even though there's no light, you can finally see everything so fucking clearly. That's what it was like with Andy #3. Finally, I was done, and not just with Andy. I was done with men leaving me unsatisfied in sexual encounters.

Andy tried to kiss me, but I turned my head, and he kissed my cheek. I turned the knob of the door and walked out. I didn't even bother to close it behind me. We never saw each other again. I wasn't interested in giving a man a fourth chance to satisfy even a single need of mine and I'm certain he had noticed the abrupt change in my attitude. Later that week, I heard back that I'd gotten the job. I was moving back to Montreal.

DATING WHILE FEMINIST

ABOUT THE AUTHOR

Writer. Dater. Masturbator. Victoria Young's debut story collection *Love Poems For Butchers* was released in 2020. Her work has also appeared in *PRISM* magazine, *Cream City Review* and (perhaps excessively) throughout the internet. She currently holds two BAs, an MA, and a whole lot of grudges. In 2016, Victoria was shortlisted for the Constance Rooke Award. Victoria first rose to "acclaim" as a sex and dating blogger and then later by holding men accountable for their shitty behavior via her Instagram posts. She's a sex positive, angry feminist, and late blooming fat activist who once had a male professor in grad school refer to her writing as Chick Lit without even a hint of awareness. He's probably dead now (fingees crossed).

Printed in Great Britain
by Amazon